WHEN WAR KNOCKS

When

War

Knocks

Kristine Kivisto

ISBN 978-1-7357262-0-5 (paperback)
ISBN 978-1-7357262-1-2 (ebook)

Library of Congress Control Number: 2020917309

First paperback edition 2020.

Cover art by Coralie Kivisto
Cover & Book design by L. Austen Johnson

www.kristinekivisto.com

For Grampa –
He loved well and was well loved.

Based on a true story.

TABLE OF CONTENTS

1

Off To War

June 1943

George and his three brothers sat around the kitchen table, heads close together as they played checkers while listening to the war news. This had been their evening ritual for the past year and a half, ever since the United States had joined the war after Pearl Harbor was attacked.

But tonight was the last night before everything was going to change.

Tomorrow, the small brown radio would still broadcast the war news into their home, sharing the updates of the American troops in their fight against Hitler and the Nazis. The checkerboard would still be spread out on the pine table in the kitchen. George would still set up the black and red checkers as soon as the evening chores were done.

But tomorrow, he would only have two brothers left to play checkers with. Because tomorrow, the family was going to say goodbye to Albert as he left on the train to go fight in the war.

Tonight, George was partnered with eighteen-year-old Albert, and together, they fought for control of the checkerboard against their oldest brother, Taavi, and youngest brother, Robert. The windows were open, letting the early summer breeze drift lazily into the house.

Father read the newspaper in his recliner near the hearth. Mother bustled about the kitchen as several of George's sisters helped with the baking. Giggles floated down the stairs, indicating a few more sisters were tucked away in their bedroom. He had six sisters in all, and with such a large family, there was hardly a moment of peace or quiet. But on a night like tonight, George was grateful for the closeness his parents and siblings provided. Try as he might, it was impossible to forget that tomorrow morning they would have to say goodbye to Albert as he went off to war.

A scratchy voice crackled through the brown speaker, the same voice that broadcast the Friday evening news into households across America. "The Allies continue to make headway in their push toward Italy. With the recent success in gaining control over several Mediterranean islands, it's only a matter of time before our troops are able to invade the mainland."

Albert paused mid-move. "I wonder if that's where I'll be heading once they give me my rifle."

George's stomach churned at the thought of Albert heading off to war. "If you could pick, where would you want to go?" he asked in a hushed whisper, keeping his voice from reaching Mother's ears.

Mother didn't like to hear or talk about anything war related. She would have preferred to keep the radio silenced. But the boys thought the war news was exciting, so instead, they kept the volume low so she couldn't hear.

"I'd like to get somewhere close enough to ol' Hitler to give him a piece of my mind, but I guess I'll have to go wherever

Uncle Sam needs me most."

Albert double-jumped his red piece over Taavi and Robert's black ones, scooped them up, and placed them on the table.

"I'd also really like to get to Finland," he said. "I could visit our grandparents, and the Finns have some fantastic military heroes. Have you ever heard of their legendary sniper?"

George shook his head.

"Are you talking about White Death?" George's thirteen-year-old sister, Eva, piped up. He hadn't noticed her sneak up to the table, but she often did—she enjoyed the war news just as much as the boys.

"Sure am. Isn't that quite the nickname? *White Death.* In one winter, he single-handedly took out over five hundred Soviets. Just bang, bang, bang!" Albert sat on the edge of the bench, moving his hands as he fired an imaginary gun. "They feared him more than war itself."

Taavi, who at twenty-four was the oldest of the siblings, spoke slowly as he moved a black checker piece. "You better be careful. When this is all over, I don't want to have to visit a headstone with your name on it on a European battlefield. And I know Mother would rather see you step off the train than be handed a folded flag and some military medals. War is serious. It's nothing to take lightly."

But Albert sat up a little straighter, and George knew he wasn't the least bit scared. "If I can make it to Finland, maybe I can talk to White Death myself and get some pointers on the best way to take out some Germans."

Father cleared his throat loudly and gave Albert a warning glance over his newspaper. Their mother worried enough about the war. She didn't need to hear Albert's plans for taking out enemy soldiers.

But Albert pressed on. "Do you really think Hitler could—"

Mother swooped into the room and switched off the radio. "Albert, that's enough." Her lips were thin, tight lines. Worry clouded her eyes. "Don't be putting ideas into these young ones' heads." She motioned to George, Robert, and Eva.

Father folded the newspaper and stood up from his chair. "Those pies smell wonderful, Aina," he said, changing the subject in an effort to keep her mind at ease. "Is it almost time for the birthday celebration?"

George's stomach fluttered. He was twelve years old today, and just as she always did on his birthday, Mother had baked two apple pies.

But this birthday felt different. The usual joy that surrounded the special day was dampened by Albert's imminent departure.

George remembered the day Albert's draft card arrived as if it had happened only moments ago. In reality, it had come in the mail several weeks ago, just days after Albert's eighteenth birthday. Mother had cried and begged him not to accept his draft notice. She said he should get a job in the copper mines like Taavi, so he could receive a deferment from the draft. Only the men with important war jobs could have an exemption from accepting their draft notices, and the copper being dug from the depths of the earth was a vital metal needed for the war effort. So, while Taavi had been able to defer his previous two draft requests, Albert was not allowed to say no.

And contrary to Mother's wishes, Albert didn't *want* to say no. He wanted to be a soldier. He was excited and proud that his country had called him to serve in the army.

Father had to constantly remind Mother that at least Uncle Sam had *some* morals—he encouraged his drafted men to finish high school before enlisting. Otherwise, Albert would have joined the army a year and a half ago, when Pearl Harbor was bombed, if Mother and Father would have let him. But neither parent would have allowed him to join before his eighteenth birthday, so he had waited.

So, while George wanted to celebrate his birthday, he couldn't quite push aside the fears creeping into his mind about Albert leaving. He watched as Mother took the apple pies out of the oven and set them on the kitchen table. Mother had saved the last two jars of canned apples for this very special June day, as no one in the family loved apple pie as much as George.

George and his brothers put away the checkers game, clearing room for the birthday celebration.

"Happy birthday, Yrjö," said George's father, addressing him by his Finnish name. George smiled as Father pronounced the name with pursed lips on the first syllable and rolled the R. It rolled smoothly off his tongue, sounding like "*Ooo-Ree-Oh*." Father often spoke in the language of his homeland, though he had immigrated to America when he was a boy. "You'll be as old as your big brothers in no time," Father added with a wink.

Then he motioned to the back door. "When we're done eating, I think they have a surprise waiting for you outside."

"Can I go before we start eating? I'll be back before you know it. The pies will still be warm."

"Of course," Father said, laughing at his young son's impatience. "Go and see what's waiting."

George dashed outside with his two older brothers as nine-year-old Robert tagged along, close at their heels. There, leaning against the barn in the corner of the backyard, was Albert's bicycle. At least, it looked like Albert's bicycle—except this one had two fully inflated tires and a sleek new coat of black paint.

"Like it?" Albert asked, bounding ahead. "The ol' Bone Shaker is yours now. I won't be needing her anymore. They don't let you take bicycles on the train when you go to war." As he said it, he stood up a little taller, and George could see the pride gleaming in his eyes.

George ran his hand over the smooth frame.

As if hearing the questions reeling in his mind, Taavi spoke. "We took the tire off my old bicycle. It's too small for me now, anyway. Swapped it for the flat on this one. And I found an old can of paint down in the copper mine the other day. Smuggled it up in my lunch pail. Go on, take it for a spin."

George flung a leg over the frame. His heart raced as he pushed the pedals around and around, making the bicycle speed forward. He pedaled through the yard, down the street, and over the railroad tracks. The wind tousled his hair. He had to squint so his eyes wouldn't water. And he felt as free as a bird on his very own bicycle.

◆ ◆ ◆

That evening, George curled up in Father's recliner as he waited for Mother to send him up to bed. He made himself as small as possible, hoping that she would overlook him and he could stay up just a few more minutes with Albert. He wished time would stop so he could stay in the cozy house, surrounded by his family, untouched by the war.

"Yrjö," Mother whispered. He startled awake, unaware that he had fallen asleep to the quiet din of conversation in the living room. "I think you should get to bed, child. We have a big day ahead of us, and you need some rest."

Mother held out her hand and pulled him from the comforts of the green fabric that smelled of sugar and flour, the residue that Father brought home every day from his job at the bakery.

George headed for the stairs but hesitated as he passed the hearth, stopping to gaze at the black-and-white photograph that was framed and displayed on the mantle. The family didn't have money to spend on luxuries, but Mother had made certain that enough pennies were set aside for one family portrait before Albert went off to war. She didn't say it out loud, but George knew she had that photograph taken so she could always remember Albert's face, in case the worst happened and he never came back.

The photograph had been taken three weeks earlier and was only developed and returned to Mother a few days ago. On the day of the portrait, the photographer had arrived with his large black camera and made the family line up in order of age, from oldest to youngest, against their two-story brown house. Father was on the left side, his arm tucked softly around Mother's shoulders. Mother wore her Sunday dress—her usual day-to-day apron was absent, the one that was always covered in flour or bits of sewing thread or soapy handprints.

Taavi stood next to Mother, dirt and grease from the copper mine covering his boots. She had pleaded for him to change his footwear, but he just laughed and told her there were more important things to worry about than clean shoes.

Next came the two oldest sisters, twenty-two-year-old Helena and twenty-year-old Elaine, who were always helping Mother run the household. But for as much as they helped around the house, they knew how to have their fair share of fun, too. When the daily chores were done, they scampered out of the house to the local park or restaurant, depending on the weather, in what Albert called their "evening mating ritual." The girls hated that term, but George always laughed. He knew that, when the time came, they would be more than capable of running their own households.

Then came Albert, standing tall and proud in his army uniform. His hair, once blond, had turned dark over the past few years. George was certain his own blond hair would eventually darken, too, just like his older siblings' hair color had changed as they grew up.

Next to Albert were the middle sisters, Ann, Catherine, and Mary, aged seventeen, sixteen, and fifteen. Mother affectionately called them her little stair children, as their blond heads were separated in height by only a few inches. If they stood side by side, they looked like a small set of steps. They were rarely found apart from one another. Even as little children, they were always stuck to each other like someone had glued their arms together.

Next in line was Eva. At thirteen, she was only a little over a year older than George. Sometimes he felt bad for Eva because she was often left out of the older girls' activities, but of all his sisters, he enjoyed her company the most. Eva was always a good partner for sharing adventures, every bit as tough and brave as the boys.

George looked at himself in the photograph. Even through the black-and-white tones, his blond hair shone brightly in the sunshine. His eyes were every bit as blue as Mother's, though in the photograph they looked light gray. He'd started a growth spurt in the past year and was now nearly as tall as Eva—and much taller than nine-year-old Robert. Robert was the last in line in the photograph. He would always be Mother's baby, no matter how much older he got. Robert was the quietest of the children, and George knew that was for the best, since he was always seeking out Mother's affection.

"My pride and joy," Mother's soft voice pulled him from his thoughts. "Look at all of you. Such wonderful children."

She squeezed his shoulders. "Now, run along. Try to get some sleep tonight."

George glanced one last time at the photograph, and then slowly climbed the stairs. He crawled into one of the two small beds in the boys' room and waited for Albert to join him. As much as he dreamed of having his own bed to sleep in every night, he would gladly continue to share if it meant his brother didn't have to go halfway around the world to fight Hitler and the Nazis.

♦ ♦ ♦

The next morning came faster than anyone would have liked. Hearts heavy and minds filled with worry, the family trudged to the train platform to see Albert off. Mother was the first to begin crying when they got to the station, and once she started, it set off a chain reaction with the sisters. They cried like a dam that had overflowed from the spring rains. Mother begged until the last minute for Albert to stay home. She said it wasn't too late—he could still apply for a job in the copper mines and receive his deferment.

But it was no use. The army officer ordered Albert up the steps, and he went. Head held high, without a tear in sight, he gave one last salute to the family and boarded the train to become a soldier.

George waved as long as he could as the train pulled out of the station and away from their town of Calumet, tucked away in the farthest northern reaches of Michigan. He didn't stop until the last car was out of sight, swallowed up by the towering pine trees on either side of the tracks.

He ducked his head and wiped his eyes on his shirt sleeve. He didn't want Taavi to see his tears, because Taavi didn't cry. George thought that maybe, by the time he was twenty-four, he would be able to stop the tears from leaking, too.

Father pulled George and Robert close, ruffling their hair. Even Father had cried. But he made sure it was after Albert had boarded the train.

The family stood solemnly on the train platform, listening as the whistle of the train grew fainter and fainter with every blast, until suddenly they could no longer hear it. Even though George had nine siblings, with Albert gone, the void in the family lineup was already apparent. Father hugged Mother. All six sisters huddled close, rubbing their eyes and wiping tears from their cheeks. George, Taavi, and Robert stood with their heads bowed and hands shoved deep into their pockets.

George felt a knot growing in his stomach, wondering when he would be able to see Albert again. He knew not every soldier who went away on that train came back. There were children from school who lost loved ones all the time. He saw the names of the fallen printed in the newspaper. The list continued to grow every week.

He closed his eyes, pressed the last of the tears from his eyelids, and hoped his brother would be safe in whatever faraway land he was headed to.

◆ ◆ ◆

"I've got something in the barn that you may like," Taavi said as the family trudged down the sidewalk in a ragged line toward home.

"What's that?" asked George, not in the mood for anything other than grabbing his fishing pole, hiding out near the riverbank, and trying to forget that Albert was on a train heading to war.

"Come on, it'll be easier to just show you."

They took the shortcut through the alley, and Taavi slid the heavy barn door open. Beams of morning sunshine filtered through cracks in the wooden walls, highlighting the dust that was floating inside. George breathed in deeply, the familiar earthen scents of the barn comforting him slightly. They lived in town, so they couldn't have any livestock, but the small barn housed their gardening supplies, various odds and ends, and an ever-rotating supply of stray cats.

Taavi walked to the back corner where his woodworking bench took up space along the wall next to the rakes and shovels. Though he was a talented woodworker, it didn't pay nearly as much as the mines. The mines were dangerous, but the money they provided was better than any other job in town—with the exception of a few distinguished positions such as a doctor or the mayor.

Taavi rummaged around in a barrel of wooden boards and dowels before pulling out a cardboard tube. "Here," he said, handing it to George. "I think this will help keep your mind busy while Albert's away. I already started it but could certainly use your help."

George tilted the cardboard cylinder straight up and down. It came up to his waist. He tapped it on the dirt floor and a rolled-up piece of paper started to slide out.

"You can put it here," Taavi motioned as he pushed his tools aside to make space.

George grabbed the large paper and flattened it the best he could. Taavi helped hold it down.

"Where'd you get this?" George asked. Spread out before them was a map of the entire world. Countries colored in green, yellow, red, and orange were nestled in great big oceans of blue. Circles, X's, and lines were drawn across borders, clearly identifying movement of some sort, though George didn't quite understand all of it.

"Had it for a while. Been keeping up with the battles and victories. We can track the Allies' progress, and providing Albert can write to us with at least a little detail of where he might be, we can make sure he's staying away from the worst of the fighting."

George ran his finger across the Atlantic Ocean. "Do you know where he will sail out of?"

"From the sounds of it," Taavi said, placing his finger on the map, "the men have been leaving New York and either going to Scotland or Algeria." He traced his finger in a wide arc across the Atlantic. "If I had money to bet, I'd put it on this route." He drew an imaginary line to Algeria, in the northern region of Africa.

"Africa?" asked George. "But I thought Hitler was in Germany."

"He is, but in order to get to Germany, our men had to fight some mighty battles that started in North Africa, and now, they are moving through the Mediterranean Sea into Italy. From there, they'll continue north to Germany and the other Nazi-occupied countries. I bet Albert will be walking through Italy in no time, but we'll have to wait for him to send a letter to be certain."

George stared at the map. It was a great big world, and it was hard to imagine Albert so far away in a strange land. But somehow, seeing the markings on Taavi's map made the war easier to understand. He was glad he had at least one big brother at home to help ease his worries.

"Take this," Taavi said, handing him a pencil. "We'll start here since we know where he left. And we know he's going to New York. We'll wait until his first letter to draw the line over the ocean. But in the meantime, we'll keep it updated with any major battles that we hear about on the radio."

George took the pencil and put a tiny star in the very northernmost part of Michigan. He then drew a dotted line down the state and heading east, to the harbors of New York City.

"That'll do for now," said Taavi. "If we listen to the war news and keep this updated, the time will pass so quickly that Albert will be back as quick as a wink."

Taavi squeezed his shoulders. "Now, run along, Yrjö. I've got to finish this bookcase for Aunt Elvie. Perhaps the fish are biting down at the river today."

George didn't have to be told twice. He grabbed his fishing pole and dashed into the woods, grateful that Taavi was able to ease some of his worries.

2

The Orphan Train
July 1943

"The orphan train is coming! The orphan train is almost here!" George shouted as he sprinted out the door into the hot July sun. "John, John, the orphan train!"

He was shouting to his best friend and neighbor, John, motioning for him to drop the ax and come to the train station. They could hear the loud whistle and see the billowing gray smoke reaching up in tall, slanted columns over the pine trees.

The trains came several times a day, every day except Sunday. They brought deliveries, people, mail, and goods. But this one was special. The noon train on this particular July Saturday was one that had been advertised for weeks. The orphans were on this one. The fliers had been posted around town and in the newspapers since spring.

"Do you still think we can get an orphan?" asked John, panting for breath as they climbed the steps to the platform and jostled to the front of the crowd.

"Hopefully," said George, equally winded. "Probably not a baby, but at least one that can walk and talk."

"I hope we aren't too late," said John, eyeing up the long line of parents waiting for the train to slow to its final stop.

The breaks hissed, popping into place. The engine let out a loud belch of soot and steam. The door of the front train car opened, and a large, heavyset woman appeared. She looked official and acted even more so.

"I bet she's the one that hands out the orphans," said George. "Come on, let's go."

The boys snaked their way closer to the large woman, who was now accompanied by a small, elderly woman.

The crowd jostled as everyone craned their necks and pushed forward to get a better view of the waiting orphans.

"Papers, please! Please have your papers ready!" the woman in charge shouted to the gathered crowd. "We will begin dispersing the children soon, but please have your papers ready. They are eager to see their new homes. Please, no pushing. You'll all be taken care of in a timely manner."

One by one, the children were brought off the train and handed to the waiting adults. There were big children and little children. Teeny babies that fussed and children who were even taller than George. All of them were in various states of emotion. Some were crying, some were happy, and some looked downright terrified. Some came with nice clothes and even the occasional satchel or suitcase of belongings. Others wore ratty and mismatched outfits. All of them had tags pinned to their clothes. The woman in charge kept looking at the tags and matching them to the paperwork handed to her by the adults on the platform.

All the adults were beaming as they were assigned a child. Some even went away with two or three children.

As the children were handed off to their new parents, the crowd thinned. George and John exchanged looks, hoping the train wasn't running out of orphans before they were able to get one.

"Ask her," John said, nudging George toward the small, old woman who was assisting in the process.

George stepped forward, tugging on her sleeve. "Excuse me, ma'am? How do we get an orphan?"

She looked at the boys with confusion, then burst into laughter.

"You can't just get an orphan," she said, still chuckling. "You had to fill out the paperwork. Weeks ago. And choose your orphan from those available. And send the money. And you also have to be a grown-up," she smiled. "We can't give children to other children."

George stood back, the stunned look on his face matching John's.

"I thought the fliers said you could get an orphan," said John. "Think we missed the instructions?"

"Must have. I didn't read anything about paperwork or sending money," replied George.

The boys stood in disappointed silence for a moment. They watched as the remaining orphans were matched with their new parents, spirits crushed they wouldn't have an orphan of their own to look after and play with—especially since they had figured if the orphan were old enough, it would have been able to help chop the mountains of firewood needed to heat their homes during the cold winter months.

Finally, the very last orphan was pulled from the train.

The boy was scrawny. His thin frame was drowned by the pants he was wearing, which were at least three sizes too big. Some kind soul had been nice enough to get him a pair of suspenders, but the pant legs were so loose the extra fabric billowed around his ankles. His clothes matched his face—filthy and smeared with dirt. His shoes were so filled with holes that he would have been better off going barefoot.

The woman in charge read his name tag and looked at the last remaining set of parents standing on the train platform. George felt ill for the scrawny orphan.

"Oh, no," John gasped, "not Mr. Olson."

Everyone in town knew of Mr. Olson. George and his friends knew better than to step foot anywhere near Mr. Olson's farm. He and his wife had gotten orphans before. Three to be exact.

The boy knew the exchange was about to take place, and he tried to wriggle free of the woman's grasp.

"Now, Will," she said sternly, "this is your new family. You have to go with them."

"No!" said the boy. "I don't want to."

Mr. Olson shoved his papers at the woman, dug his fingers into Will's shoulder, and tore him from her grip.

"Doesn't matter what you want, son," boomed Mr. Olson. "You're my boy now, and you'll listen to me."

George and John watched in horror, hearing Will's useless protests as he was dragged off the train platform and shoved into the back of Mr. Olson's automobile. His wife squeezed into the passenger seat, a smug smile plastered on her face.

"I bet she's really glad to have another orphan," said George.

"For sure," said John, "she won't have to do chores anymore. Just gets to sit around and let the boy do all the work."

"Think he'll figure out what happened to the other three orphans?" asked George.

John didn't answer. They weren't sure if knowing would be better or worse for Will. Rumors had flown all over school that the last Olson orphans had ended up dead and buried in their swamp.

George hoped Will wouldn't have the same fate.

◆ ◆ ◆

After a sullen walk home, George's mother shooed them back to town to Mr. Jenkins's grocery store to see if the shipment of butter had arrived. Often, due to fuel and food shortages, they weren't able to get their monthly ration of butter on time.

George held the book of ration stamps in his hand as he and John walked barefoot down the cement sidewalk to the grocery store. The ration book had just been replenished, but just because they had stamps, it didn't mean they were guaranteed the food.

Due to the war, every family had a ration book. It limited them to certain quantities of food for the month, since so much food was needed overseas to feed the soldiers. But often, there were food shortages, and the items just weren't available at Mr.

Jenkins's store. George hoped today's shipment had arrived. Meals were so much better with sweet, salted butter.

A bicycle whizzed past, then screeched to a halt as the rider skidded to a stop, leaving a thin, black tire mark on the sidewalk.

"Not today," George groaned under his breath. It was Ricky McClain. Showing off again on his new bicycle. Making fun of George every chance he got.

"Hey, George," Ricky taunted, "going to get some handouts like a vulture? Maybe you should try the department store next. I hear they're having a sale today. Shoes are half off for the poor folks."

George shuffled his bare feet on the cement sidewalk, fists balled up at his sides as he wished Ricky would ride away. He knew better than to let Ricky see his anger. Plus, he knew the teasing shouldn't make him mad. He had shoes at home. They may be hand-me-downs from his two older brothers, but he did have shoes. And they fit him perfectly fine. But it was summer now, so he went barefoot to keep the wear and tear on his shoes to a minimum. There was still one more younger brother at home who needed to use the shoes.

"Bug off, Ricky," said John.

"I heard the grocery store is empty today. Nothing left—not even a can of beans," Ricky shouted with glee as he hopped back on his bicycle and sped down the sidewalk.

George took a step in Ricky's direction, but John grabbed his arm. "Don't worry about him. He's not worth your time."

But John didn't understand the humiliation that Ricky

brought to George. George hated that he couldn't retaliate. And he hated that Ricky didn't know what it felt like to live without luxuries. Ricky's father was rich. He owned Mineshaft Number Five, where George's oldest brother and many of the men from town worked in dangerous, and often deadly, conditions. Even in these times of shortage, Ricky's family always had enough. George doubted they followed their book of ration stamps, the evidence of that being Ricky's perpetually too-tight pants.

George clutched the ration book tightly in his hands. He wished he could chase after Ricky and take some stamps from his family's ration book. He knew they didn't need all those stamps. And with nine children still at home in George's house and only one at Ricky's, certainly they could spare some of the more sought-after items.

"Let's go," said John, pulling him back to reality. "Maybe Jenkins got that butter delivery after all."

3

The Abandoned Mine
July 1943

"Mother, what's for lunch?" George asked as he banged through the back door. His birch branch fishing pole was secured in the barn, and the hunger in his stomach was beginning to gnaw.

"Sandwiches in the fridge," said his oldest sister, Helena, intercepting the question. She wiped her brow, sweat dampening the bangs on her forehead.

George stuck his head into the kitchen and immediately pulled back from the heat.

"Laundry day already?" he asked as his mother and six sisters bustled about the room. The day was hot, yet a fire blazed in the hearth. A large black kettle filled with hot, soapy water was suspended on a black iron hook over the flames.

"Once a week, Yrjö. Same as it's always been," Mother smiled, ruffling his hair with a damp hand. "What have you been up to this morning?"

"Fishing with John. Didn't catch anything. Flies got too bad."

"Ah, well, you better get back outside. I don't want more people suffering in this heat than need be," she said, opening the refrigerator and pushing a thick ham and cheese sandwich into his hands.

George grabbed the sandwich, dashed into the cellar for some canned strawberries, and headed back out into the bright sunshine. Even though it was hot outside, it wasn't nearly as miserable as the humid kitchen where the laundry needed to be soaked, scrubbed, rinsed, and then hung outside on the clothesline. Some of the wealthy folks in town had newfangled washing machines to ease the laundry burden. He hoped Mother would be able to get one someday.

John made his way outside. Their houses sat side-by-side and backed up to a small grove of apple trees at the lot line. The boys sat under the shade of the trees, enjoying their lunches.

"Look," said George, pointing at the small yellow fruit hanging overhead. "They'll be red and ripe in no time. Looks like it'll be a bumper crop this year."

"I can't wait for cider," said John.

"And pie," said George, his mouth already watering. "We ate the last of our apples last month. I wish they were ripe year-round."

"Me, too, but at least the blueberries will be ready for picking soon."

"Do you think your father will bring us to the blueberry patch again?" asked George. His thoughts turned back to the fun week they had last year when John's father had driven them to Rice Lake. They had slept in a canvas tent, fished in the lake, and brought home pail upon pail of fresh, wild blueberries for their families.

"I'll ask. The berries should be getting ripe soon."

The boys were dreaming of their possible adventure when a movement on the sidewalk at the end of the alley caught their attention. A well-dressed man was hurrying down Pine Street, his hunched form slipping out of view behind the lilac bushes.

"Oh, no," John said. "I wonder where he's going."

"As long as it's not here. Anywhere but here," George replied. A pit of icy cold filled his stomach as he imagined what a visit from the well-dressed man would mean.

The Western Union man reappeared from his cover of the lilac bushes, and they watched as he hurried out of view, a yellow telegram clutched tightly in his hand. All the people in town knew of him, and all dreaded his visits. He delivered telegrams sharing news of the soldiers fighting in the war.

Telegrams were faster than letters, and they always seemed to contain bad news, such as someone missing in action. Worst of all, they brought news that a soldier had died. It was the Western Union man's job to relay the news. George could not think of a worse job to have.

Shaking the uneasy feeling from their minds, John suggested a plan for how to spend the remainder of the afternoon.

"What do you think about trying to find that old mine crosscut that Albert told you about?"

"Sure," said George. "Only this time, we have to go farther down the hill. Taavi said we were looking too high up on the ridge. It's closer to the bottom, near the creek."

George finished up his lunch and ran inside to grab Taavi's old mining helmet from the cellar. He flicked the switch, and the light shone brightly, indicating the batteries still worked.

He quietly slipped out the back door, making sure not to alert anyone as to where he was going.

Mother was always warning the children to stay away from the old mines. They were damp and dark, and one wrong step could send a person plummeting deep into the earth with no way out.

But to George and John, the mines were a wonderful place to explore. Before Albert left on the train to go to war, he had told George about the abandoned mine crosscut a few miles north of town. It connected Mineshafts Number Two and Number Five, but the end of the tunnel had collapsed a few years back, and the mining company decided it wasn't worth the effort to clean up the rockfall.

The boys had searched for the mine a couple of weeks ago but couldn't find it. Now, with the wind blowing through their hair, they sped on their bicycles down the hill to the winding, shallow creek at the bottom. It didn't take long, and following Taavi's instructions, they headed upstream to the place where two pine trees leaned over the river from opposite banks, creating an X.

George crouched, crawling under some fallen branches at the bottom of the cliff. The boys rounded a bend, and there, hidden behind a pile of loose boulders, was the opening to the mine crosscut.

"I'll go first," said George, flicking the switch on his helmet. A strong beam of light swept across the cavernous floor when he looked from left to right and back again.

"Careful. Watch for holes and cave-ins," warned John.

The boys stepped deeper and deeper into the chilly tunnel. Water dripped from above, plunking into puddles on the stone floor. Their feet quickly became cold, and their pant legs were soaked from the damp cave system.

"Think there are any bears in here?" whispered John. "Seems like it would be the perfect place for bears."

"No, it's July. Bears are out picking berries. Not in caves."

But as he said it, the hairs on the back of George's neck stood up.

Even though the light was bright, he couldn't see very far in front of him. The mine tunnel had all sorts of turns and cutouts that were blocked from his view. He inched forward, unsure of what creatures lurked ahead.

They went on, disturbing a swarm of bats that were clinging to the rocky ceiling.

"Ahhh!" screamed the boys, dropping to the floor as the bats swooped overhead and flapped their wings in the direction of the entrance.

George stood up, his light swinging to the side of the tunnel before shining on a dark lump. It was the indistinguishable form of a cave creature huddled in the darkness. The creature stirred, then began to move.

"Run!" he screamed at John, turning around. In his haste, he knocked John over, and they both crashed into a puddle of water on the cold, rocky floor.

Laughter echoed down the walls of the cave, and the boys screamed again.

"Help!" yelled John. "Help! Run!"

Just then, George's light went out, and they were plunged into complete darkness.

♦ ♦ ♦

A flashlight flicked on, bathing the mine tunnel in a soft glow.

"Scared?" a small voice called from the side of the cave. Its laughter had now stopped.

"It's the orphan!" gasped George.

"What are you doing here?" asked John.

The two boys stared at the third, who was crouched against the wall of the tunnel and wrapped in a scraggly wool blanket. His bare feet stuck out from beneath the fringe of the material. A black eye was visible, even in the dim light. He had scratches on his arms and face, and if George had to guess, probably on his legs, too.

"Are you okay?" George asked the scrawny boy.

"Better than I was two days ago," the boy replied. A small smile tugged at the corners of his mouth.

"Who gave you that shiner? Was it mean old Mr. Olson?" asked John.

The boy nodded. "He ain't my father, though. That's for sure."

"What happened to Mr. Olson's other orphans?" asked John.

"Were they really dead and buried in the swamp?"

George nudged John in the ribs to stop him from asking any more ridiculous questions.

"Dunno about any other orphans," said the boy. "But I ain't going back. Found me this old mine tunnel. It's pretty cozy in here, to be honest."

The orphan motioned to his small sack of belongings. George guessed what little food he had was stolen from Mrs. Olson's pantry and smuggled out as he ran away.

"How about you come home with us?" George offered the boy. "My mother can fix you up. That eye needs a good cleaning and some medicine."

The boy reached up, gingerly touching his injury. Dried blood outlined a cut where a heavy fist had split his skin open.

"You'll get an infection," said John, "especially living in this damp cave."

But the orphan boy was stubborn. "Nah, I like it here. It's quiet. I don't have to hear anyone yell at me. And besides, I need some rest. Been worked nearly to the bone this past week."

George and John stood in front of the injured, wet, and tired orphan boy.

"Can we at least bring you some supplies?" asked George, not wanting to leave the boy alone in a place where death could so easily find him.

"Do what you wish, but I ain't begging for nothing."

◆ ◆ ◆

George and John sped back home on their bicycles. John was in charge of getting food, and George was tasked with sneaking the medicine out of his mother's cabinet. He crept through the house, into his mother's bedroom, and secured the small jar of ointment in his pocket before any of his sisters figured out that he was up to something. Then, he ran upstairs into his bedroom and grabbed two clean handkerchiefs from Albert's drawer to help cover the wounds.

He met John in the backyard, and they hopped back on their bicycles. They raced down the hill again, eager to deliver their supplies to the orphan.

4

Operation: Rescue Will
August 1943

George was awake early and could hear Taavi getting ready for work downstairs.

Father was already long gone. He always left in the wee hours of the morning for his job at the bakery. He had worked there ever since settling in the town after he moved to America. The bread, rolls, and pastries needed to be mixed early so the dough could rise and be baked before the morning crowd showed up, so it was very rare that anyone in the family saw him in the mornings.

George waited under the covers until he heard the back door close. Then, he slipped out of bed, avoided the squeaky floorboards, skipped over the creaky steps, and carefully made his way downstairs.

It had been three days since he had found the orphan boy, and it was time to bring him more supplies.

"What are you doing?" a voice hissed, cutting through the early morning silence.

George spun around, startled at the sudden and unexpected witness.

"What are you doing? Put that food back. Where are you going?" His older sister, Mary, stood in front of him, hands on her hips so he couldn't escape the pantry.

"Shh," George motioned to his lips, not wanting to wake the rest of the family.

"You *shh*," she mocked. "What are you doing?"

"Can't tell you."

"Yes, you can."

"No, I can't."

"Yes, you will. Or I'll go get Mother and tell her you're stealing food."

George looked Mary in the eyes. She was not joking.

"What are you doing awake, anyway?" he deflected.

"Outhouse," she motioned to the back door. "Now, what are *you* doing?"

George hesitated. He didn't want to tell, but he also knew Mary wasn't going to let it go.

"We found an orphan. Me and John. He was Mr. Olson's. But Mr. Olson beat him up, so now, he's hiding in the abandoned mine crosscut. The one between Mineshafts Two and Five."

Mary's eyes widened in fear. "The one Albert told you about? The one that Mother said you should never, ever, *ever* explore?"

George nodded, his stomach churning now that he had spilled his secret to Mary, the best rule follower in the entire family.

"Please don't tell Mother," George begged. "His name is Will. He came to town on the train the other week. He doesn't want to go back to Mr. Olson."

"Well, you tell Will that he can't live in a cave forever. Besides, it'll be downright miserable when winter comes."

"I know. And he knows. He just has to get better. Then he said he's going to hop on the first train out of town and live with the hobos traveling west."

Mary stared at George, dropping her hands from her waist so he wasn't trapped in the pantry anymore.

"Here," she said, her voice calming down as she reached up to the highest shelf. "At least take him this."

She shoved a loaf of fresh bread into George's burlap sack. It nestled down next to the small bag of peanuts, an almost empty jar of peanut butter, and five hard-boiled eggs.

"*Kiitos*," he said. *Thank you.*

"You're welcome. Please be careful. And don't worry, I won't tell Mother. She has enough on her mind right now."

♦ ♦ ♦

George and John cruised on their bicycles through the early morning mist. John had a large jug of fresh water and a long spool of gauze for Will's wounds. They were hopeful that the ointment was making progress from its first application a few days ago.

"Think he's still there?" asked John as they dropped their bicycles in the ditch on the side of the road and made their way up the creek to the opening of the mine crosscut.

"Guess there's only one way to find out," George responded as he flicked on his helmet light, now with a fresh pair of batteries to power it.

The boys sloshed through the soggy tunnel, pant legs rolled up to escape the moisture.

"Will?" George called out. "Will?"

His voice echoed down the cavernous tunnel, sounding like several Georges were calling out for several Wills.

"Mornin'," came a sleepy voice, quickly followed by the click of his flashlight. The mine tunnel was once again flooded in soft light.

The boys presented Will with their goods, and he ravenously dug into the food. He barely stopped for breath as he inhaled three hard-boiled eggs, the entire bag of peanuts, half of the loaf of bread, and then began eating the peanut butter straight from the jar with his fingers.

"Hungry?" asked John.

Will nodded. "Glad you came back! Ate the last of Mrs. Olson's food yesterday morning. Wasn't quite sure what I was going to do today."

The boys waited in silence, letting Will enjoy the sweet peanut butter as he scooped the remainder from the jar.

"I guess we can't wait three days between trips," said George.

"Or we'll have to bring more food next time," said John before turning back to Will. "By the way, how's the shiner?"

Will peeled the handkerchiefs from his head. The boys leaned in. Even in the dim light, they could see the wound already looked much better.

"Let's get you cleaned up and put some fresh medicine on that," said George.

They used water and a clean handkerchief to wash the wound. Then, Will applied a new layer of ointment, and George helped him cover it with fresh gauze.

"So, how'd you end up on that train, anyway?" John asked as he put the lid back on the ointment.

"Ain't a story I care to bother you with," mumbled Will.

"Come on, we want to know," urged John.

"Yeah," agreed George. "Please?"

Will sat and fiddled with some peanut shells scattered on the hard earth in front of him.

The boys waited in silence, not wanting to leave the mine until they had heard Will's story.

Finally, he spoke. "My pa done up 'n' died on us. Caught the fever from a ship that sailed in from the East. He worked down at the docks—north side of Chicago. Ma didn't waste no time. Pa was barely cold, and she'd already married a fella by the name of Dunlop, though me and my brothers just called him Wallop 'cause that's what he did to us all day, anyway.

"He wouldn't give us no food, no nothin'. Mad as a hornet as long as the sun shone. His two girls got our bedroom. Me and my brothers had to sleep on the wood planks in the parlor. One day, James tried to beat up ol' Mr. Wallop, but he got licked real good. He got his nose broke, his arm broke, and landed himself smack dab in the hospital.

"Ma was none too happy about any of it. She seemed to have lost her marbles by then, with Pa dying 'n' all. Maybe the fever got to her head the same way it got to Pa's lungs. I reckon I'll never know. Next thing I knew, she had all three of us lined up for photographs and sent us away on that orphan train. Just dropped us off in ol' Wallop's truck and never looked back."

Will was stacking the peanut shells on top of each other, a small mound now formed on the ground.

"I'm sorry to hear that," George whispered.

"No kidding," John agreed, eyes wide as he stared at Will. "I wouldn't have asked had I known it was that bad. Do you know what happened to your brothers?"

"I reckon they probably made it somewhere by now," Will shrugged. "Hopefully, someplace better than where I ended up."

"You sure you don't want to come live at my house?" asked George.

"I'm sure. I'll be fine in here for a while. It's been a long time since I had some peace 'n' quiet." He leaned back against the stone wall. "Now, you best be gettin' on with your day. I don't want your folks worryin' to your whereabouts."

◆ ◆ ◆

George and John pedaled home, hands and pockets now empty.

"Wanna race?" asked John.

In response, George sped up as they approached a large downhill. "You'll never win!" he yelled, squinting his eyes to keep them from watering.

The boys were neck and neck, nearing the bottom of the hill

at top speed. They were almost to the curve when a delivery truck came barreling around the bend, unsuspecting that two boys would be racing their bicycles in the early morning hour.

"Look out!" yelled John as he veered to the right, dodging the truck.

George followed suit, only to hit a gravel patch on the side of the road. The bicycle was going too fast to control. He tumbled into the ditch and launched it down the embankment and into some brush.

He tried to catch his breath but was left crouched low after the wind had been knocked clean out of his lungs. He gasped for air, pain radiating from fresh scrapes on his knees, legs, and elbows.

The delivery truck screeched to a halt, the driver rushing over to check on the boys.

"You okay?" the driver asked, bending down to help George to his feet.

"I'm okay," George gasped, holding back tears as his exposed, raw skin screamed for attention.

"Wasn't expecting you boys to come tearing down that hill so fast." The driver scrambled into the ditch to retrieve the busted-up bicycle from the trees.

George looked at the broken bicycle, and his stomach sank. He had barely had it two months, and already, the tire was bent and the frame was scratched. He wondered if Taavi would be able to help him fix it.

"Looks like you boys need a ride now. Hop in," the driver

motioned.

The boys climbed into the bed of the truck, surrounded by John's working bicycle, George's broken bicycle, and scratchy burlap sacks of grain. The truck turned around, heading back toward town with a new delivery added to its route.

◆ ◆ ◆

"Ouch, Yrjö," said George's mother. "What on earth happened? What were you doing on your bicycle so early in the morning?"

George bit his lip, partly to keep from saying anything, and partly to keep from crying out in pain as she dabbed antiseptic on his wounds.

"Mary, go grab me the ointment from my bedroom cabinet," she said as she finished cleaning the dirt from his skin.

George's stomach turned. The ointment was still in the mine crosscut with Will.

"It's not here, Mother," came Mary's voice from the bedroom.

"Are you sure? I just had it the other day. What could have come of it?"

"I bet George knows where it is," Mary said, returning to view with a gleam in her eyes, hinting that she wanted to tell Mother the secret of what George had been up to.

"George, do you know where the ointment is?" his mother asked.

"Um, well, I guess, not really. . . ." He stumbled over his words, not wanting to risk Will's newfound safety in the mine.

"George?" Mother asked again, her voice rising in pitch as worried creases formed between her eyes.

Mary interrupted, unable to keep the secret any longer. "It's with the orphan boy. In the crosscut."

"What orphan boy? What crosscut?"

"He's been going to see the orphan boy. The one that ran away from Mr. Olson's place. He's living in the abandoned mine crosscut near Old Colony Creek."

"George," his mother said, color draining from her face, "have you been going into the mine tunnels?"

George nodded, unable to look her in the eyes.

She began mumbling in her native Finnish tongue. She often spoke in the language of her homeland when she became upset or worried.

Finally, she returned to English and demanded, "George, you will wait inside today until your father gets home from work. Then, you will go with him to the mine, and he will bring the orphan boy back here. Once the child is clean and fed, we will have to return him to his rightful guardian, Mr. Olson."

"But, Mother!" George felt the panic rising in his chest. "He's not safe there. Mr. Olson is a mean old man. You know that just as well as anyone else."

Mother stood in silence for a moment, her fingers tracing the embroidery on the pocket of her apron. When she spoke, her voice was soft. "I'm sorry, Yrjö. As much as I'd like to keep him, I know Mr. Olson would have the sheriff knocking on our door the minute he heard Will was living here. Besides, our ration stamps are stretched thin enough. I'm sure Will would get heartier meals at the Olson farm."

George knew it was no use arguing with Mother. And she was right. It would only be a matter of time before Mr. Olson heard that Will was living with them. The town was small, and gossip spread quicker than wildfire.

He waited for what felt like an eternity for Father to get home from working at the bakery so they could get Will. His stomach was in knots the entire time as he listened for the familiar tread of Father's boots up the back steps. But his mind was racing, scheming of a way to keep Will from having to go back to Mr. Olson's.

5

The Blueberry Patch
August 1943

The war rations on gas and rubber made it too expensive for George's family to own an automobile. And with both his and Taavi's bicycles in various states of disrepair, George and his father had to make the trip to retrieve Will on foot.

It was a long walk to the mine crosscut and back again. Father led the way home, closely followed by the two barefoot boys. Will had given up on his tattered shoes and tossed them in his burlap sack before they left the mine. They eventually made their way down Pine Street into town. John's house came into view first since it sat squarely on the corner lot. Next to it was George's two-story brown house.

"Run inside now, boys," said Father, "and listen to Mother."

George and Will trudged up the steps, both wishing they could be back in the familiar, damp mine tunnel and safe from the incoming onslaught of questions.

"Oh, you poor thing." Mother descended on Will as soon as they pushed the back door open. Her hands were immediately busy as she took his small sack of belongings and placed it on the kitchen table. She pulled the bandages from his head, her fingers gently prodding his wound to check for any sign of infection.

"Mary, Helena," she called to the girls, "bring me towels and washcloths, and please go find something from Albert's closet for the boy to wear. Will, let's get you cleaned up and comfortable."

Will's eyes darted around the room, taking in the busy household. George was certain that Will hadn't been fussed over to such an extent in recent years. Yet, he seemed to be enjoying the attention.

George stood in the kitchen, leaning against the counter as he watched his mother and sisters bustle about. They ordered Will into the washroom to bathe, then gathered clothes and medicine while beginning to prepare a warm supper.

Once Will was in the bathtub, the sisters began to interrogate George.

"How did you find Will?" asked Helena, his oldest sister.

"Do you have any idea how angry Mr. Olson must be?" asked sixteen-year-old Catherine.

"Is he really going to ride the train with the hobos?" asked Eva, ever the most adventurous of the sisters.

"No," interrupted Mother in a stern voice, "he's going back to Mr. Olson's. There will be no more talk of hobos or trains."

The room was silent for a moment, broken by Ann. "Think Will's going to end up dead and buried in the swamp, like the other orphans?"

"Ann!" scolded Elaine. "Stop scaring the poor boy. He can probably hear you!"

George's younger brother, Robert, ambled into the room, staying out of view but still able to listen to the conversation about the fate of the orphan. They had never had a real live runaway orphan in their house. This was the most excitement the family had experienced in ages.

The questions continued faster than George could answer. He began to think this must be what prisoners of war felt like. He was being forced to answer questions he didn't know the answers to.

Finally, Father and Taavi entered the house, and supper was transferred from the stove to the table. Will finished bathing and got dressed in some of Albert's clothes, which dwarfed him just like the pair of pants he had worn when he got off the orphan train.

"Hmm," said Mother, pinching and tugging the fabric with her fingers. "After supper, I'll bring this in a little here, make that a little smaller there, and hem those pants a good four inches."

Mother was an excellent seamstress. The family didn't have extra money to buy new clothes, so the ones they did have needed to last as long as possible. That meant plenty of hand-me-downs, alterations, and mending. Mother also took in additional sewing jobs from the townsfolk as a way to earn money. She was well-known around town for her sewing skills.

George was certain that the clothes would fit his new orphan friend perfectly before the evening was over.

♦ ♦ ♦

As the boys climbed the stairs to bed that night, their minds were racing. Will was still set to be taken back to Mr. Olson's in the morning. Mother had wanted to do it that evening, but George had convinced her to let Will have at least one night in a warm bed before leaving.

"You really think this plan is going to work?" asked Will, his voice full of worry.

"It's our best option. Unless you want to go back to Mr. Olson's. And to be honest, riding the train with a bunch of hobos isn't exactly the safest."

George and Will crawled into bed and stared at the ceiling, wide awake, waiting for the long hours to pass. The noise downstairs slowly dwindled. Soon, all the girls were in their bedroom, soft giggles escaping now and again. In the boys' bedroom, Taavi's sleepy snores were the first to fill the room, Robert's following closely behind.

The occupants in the bed across the room were now oblivious to the escape plan about to be underway.

George could hear Father's heavy footsteps performing their nightly routine. A trip to the outhouse. A quick stop in the washroom. The click of the radio as it returned to its silent state. Then the footsteps shuffled into the downstairs bedroom, where the bed groaned as Father climbed in for the night.

Mother's soft footsteps stayed active a while longer. She finished the last of the dishes and put away the remaining clean linens, now dry from their afternoon spent hanging on the clothesline. But soon enough, even she crawled into bed.

The boys lay still. From their vantage point, they could see out the bedroom window. The moon was bright, nearly full. That would help Will in his travels tonight. They watched it traverse slowly across the sky. Finally, once it was nearing the edge of the far pane, George knew it was time to go.

"Ready?" he whispered.

Will sat up in response, and the boys crept out of the bedroom and down the steps. George grabbed Will's burlap sack and filled it with a few slices of bread, some cheese, and a large canteen of water.

They tiptoed out the back door and into the darkness. George walked as far as the end of Pine Street with Will before bidding him goodnight.

"Remember, you just have to get to the bottom of the hill on the road to Rice Lake. We'll be coming by mid-morning. Pretend you're a hitchhiker. We'll get John's father to stop. You can stay near Oakley's bend for the rest of the night. The washout left that cabin deserted. Just don't go upstairs. The floorboards are all rotten, and you might fall through. Good luck and see you soon."

Will slipped away into the night. The moonlight bathed his small form as he walked across the main highway toward the trail in the woods that would take him where he needed to be, come morning.

♦ ♦ ♦

John was in the front seat, George was in the back, and their gear was stowed in the trunk as John's father drove them away from town on Saturday morning in his black automobile. It had been a long night of waiting. George hadn't slept a wink.

The boys were eager to begin their adventure into the blueberry patch for a week, and even more anxious to see if Will had managed to get to the Rice Lake road so they could pick him up.

So far, the plan had gone well. If Mother had suspected George of helping Will escape, she hadn't said a word. When George slunk downstairs in the morning without Will, she hadn't pressed the issue. He figured it was for the best. Fewer questions on both ends meant less dishonesty. He didn't want to have to lie to her. But she did hum a tune as she brewed the morning coffee. George sang along to the hymn as he stirred a spoonful of brown sugar into his oatmeal.

Love came down
And rescued me
Love came down
And set me free

George wondered if perhaps his mother was breathing her own sigh of relief since she didn't have to send Will back to Mr. Olson's farm.

But now, sitting in the automobile, the boys fixed their eyes on the road ahead as they looked for Will waiting on the side of the road. If they could get him into the automobile and out to the blueberry patch, they could easily get him to his final destination, Old Widower Robinson's cabin.

The boys craned their necks as they approached the bottom of Rice Lake hill, scanning the road ahead for a boy with a burlap sack.

"What in the . . ." John's father mumbled as they sped along the road.

"Pa, stop!" John hollered. "A hitchhiker. Let's see where he's going."

"That's not a hitchhiker; that's a boy," John's father muttered to himself as he slowed the automobile to a stop.

"Hey, son," he hollered out the open window, "where are you heading?"

"Rice Lake," said Will, a sly smile lighting up his face.

"Hop in. That's too far for a young lad to be walking on a hot day."

Will yanked the back door open and slid into the seat next to George. They exchanged grins but not words. John's father didn't know about Will, the runaway orphan, so it was best not to raise any suspicion.

♦ ♦ ♦

The boys arrived at their camping destination, waved to John's father as he pulled back onto the road, and began whooping and cheering.

"We did it! We got you back!" George said, giving Will a high five.

"No more Mr. Olson!" John danced in circles, grinning.

"Freedom," said Will, a grateful smile lighting up his face.

The boys pitched their canvas tent under a large oak tree a

hundred yards from the road. They grabbed their pocketknives, quickly whittled branches into fishing poles, and headed to the lake in search of fresh fish for supper. They spent the rest of the day fishing, figuring there would be plenty of time to pick blueberries in the week ahead.

That night, as the Milky Way sparkled high above their heads, they threw log after log into the fire. Sleep was the last thing on their minds, and they enjoyed the fact that no parent was going to come out into the woods to remind them to brush their teeth and go to bed.

George and Will were tossing a pine cone back and forth over the fire, trying to break their record of three hundred twenty-nine consecutive catches. John was busy whittling, turning birch branches into guns.

"Did you hear about our boys' latest victory?" asked John. "It just came over the radio this morning. They're calling it the Battle of Vella Gulf. My pa told me six American destroyers in the South Pacific sank three Japanese destroyers. Bam! Bam! Bam! He said over a thousand Japs died, but not one single American was killed. Can you believe that?"

"Betcha them sharks went away fat and happy after that feast," Will mused as he tossed the pine cone back to George.

"I bet sharks love a fresh Jap for supper," said John as he aimed his partially finished gun into the dark woods, checking the sights.

But George remained silent. The war was still a faraway fantasy for John and Will. John just had three younger sisters, so no one in his family had to go away on the train to fight. And Will didn't exactly have a family anymore, so his worries were on things other than his loved ones dying in battle. But George knew it could just as easily have been Albert who was killed. He shivered, wondering if his brother had made it across the Atlantic yet.

"Right, George? George?"

"Huh? What?" George was pulled from his thoughts.

John was talking to him. "I was just saying we should probably get some sleep so we can get started filling those pails with blueberries in the morning. Ma would be none too happy if we came home with a bucket of fish and no berries."

So, just as pink tendrils were snaking into the eastern sky, the three boys crawled into the canvas tent to get some rest.

♦ ♦ ♦

"I suspect Ma will be happy as a lark with this haul," John said as he leaned against the oak tree where nearly two dozen buckets of blueberries were resting in the thick shade.

The boys were stretched out under the tree enjoying the morning. They were down to their last few hours of freedom before John's father came to pick them up in the afternoon. They had enjoyed a wonderful week in the wilderness. They had fished every morning, picked pail after pail of delicious ripe blueberries, swam in the lake to pass the time during the hot afternoons, sat around the campfire every night, and slept in their canvas tent under the stars.

"I suppose we should get to Old Widower Robinson's," said George, initiating the final phase of their plan for Will's escape. "It's a bit of a walk from here."

The boys helped Will pack his meager sack of belongings, and they walked down the dirt path that headed west, away from the blueberry patch. They could smell the cabin before they could see it. The woodstove sent a tall column of pale smoke into the calm blue sky.

"Howdy," George called to Old Widower Robinson, who was chopping wood in preparation for the long winter ahead.

"What in tarnation are you three boys doing way out here?" he asked, dropping his ax and leaning against the woodshed.

"Are you still looking for a boy?" asked George, not wasting any time in explaining their mission.

He knew the widower was looking for a helper. George's father had mentioned it earlier in the summer after Widower Robinson had stopped in the bakery. The widower was getting old now, and since his wife and three children had died in a house fire many years back, he had led a secluded life on the outskirts of town.

"I sure am. Whatcha got for me?"

"This is Will," George motioned to his friend. "He needs a home. You got room for him?"

Old Widower Robinson looked Will up and down. The boys held their breath. If this part of their plan failed, they were back to square one, and Will would either end up at Mr. Olson's or on a dangerous train headed west with the hobos.

Finally, the widower spoke. "Can you swing an ax?"

Will nodded.

"Know how to fish?"

Will nodded.

"Shovel snow?"

Will nodded.

"Help in the garden?"

Will nodded.

"Is he a mute boy?" the old man asked George.

"N—no, sir," stammered Will, finding his voice. "Not at all. I'm strong. I'll work hard. Just need a place to stay. I can work in the garden, fish, pick berries, clean, and even do a little cooking."

"Then, welcome home," said Old Widower Robinson, walking toward the boys with his arm outstretched. He shook Will's hand while clapping him on the shoulder. "Glad to have you. Been getting mighty lonely out here these days. And with my leg acting up, it'll be good to have an extra set of hands."

George and John left Will and three pails of blueberries with Old Widower Robinson. As they turned and walked away from the clearing in the woods, they heard a voice call out.

"I almost forgot," Will hollered from the woodpile where he had already taken control of the ax. "Thanks for everything! I certainly owe you both. And tell your ma I appreciate her fixin' me up so good."

"Don't mention it," George waved, a bittersweet feeling settling in his chest.

He walked back down the path with John, and together they

sat beneath the oak tree to wait for John's father to pick them up and bring them home. Finally, a black automobile bumped down the dirt road, hauling behind it a large cloud of dust. They loaded their belongings and berries into the trunk. They wanted to tell John's father how happy Will was to have a new home but knew they couldn't spill the secret. It wasn't worth the risk of Mr. Olson finding out where Will had gone.

6

Victory Starts at Home
August 1943

George pedaled his newly repaired bicycle through the town streets. It was a lazy, mid-August day. The summer humidity was testing the patience of even the most docile creatures. Stray dogs kept hidden in the shadows of trees. Horses tied to the hitching posts flicked at pesky flies with their tails. Deliverymen wiped their brows as they dropped off heavy loads to the stores on Fifth Street.

George thought of the blueberries that he had picked with John and Will the other week. They were now canned and put away in the cool cellar to last for the winter. He would give just about anything to put a handful of the juicy fruit over a cold scoop of vanilla ice cream and eat it in the shade of the apple trees in his backyard. But ice cream was another luxury the war had taken from them.

"Stupid war," he mumbled to himself as he avoided a pothole and crossed the street toward the salvage yard.

Posters had been hung up throughout the town over the past few weeks. They were in store windows, on the train platforms, and even in the notice boxes tacked to the lampposts. The notices were from Uncle Sam. He had another request, this time for those not able to fight in his war. The posters asked the townsfolk to recycle materials that could be made into products to help win the war. George helped out as much as he could. For the past few weeks, he had been going from house to house on his bicycle, gathering tin cans and scrap metal to turn in for the war effort. Every bit helped, but he wished he could do more. He knew that a few armfuls of scrap metal would hardly make a dent in all the supplies the soldiers needed. There were just too many war materials needed, and a few tin cans would only stretch so far. Still, he did what he could to help.

After turning in his scrap metal from the past week of collecting, he pedaled back down Fifth Street while dreaming of cold ice cream and crisp soda. He wiped his brow, coming to terms with the fact that he'd have to quench his cravings with some ice water instead.

As he coasted down a small hill, he came to the printshop for the Finnish newspaper called *The Suomi Times,* which George's father subscribed to. Since many of the people in town were immigrants, they often bought newspapers in the languages of their homelands. There were newspaper shops throughout town that printed in Finnish, Swedish, Norwegian, Polish, Croatian, Italian, and more.

Though the English newspapers often brought faster and more accurate news of the happenings in the States, they didn't touch on anything happening back in Finland, where George's grandparents and many relatives still lived.

Gurney Mills, the owner of *The Suomi Times*, sat on the

outdoor steps smoking a pipe.

"Hi, Gurney," said George, skidding to a halt over the bumpy sidewalk. An idea had popped into his head.

"G'afternoon, George," said Gurney, puffing a cloud of smoke from his lips as he spoke.

George looked at Gurney's ink-stained hands. "You're hiring?" he asked, nodding to the white sign that was propped up in the window.

"Sure am. Do you want to deliver? I need another carrier on Tuesdays and Thursdays."

"Yes, I do!"

"Well, then, you're hired. You can do the morning route. Be here at eight."

"I'll be here," said George, hopping back onto his bicycle before pausing a moment. "And Gurney? What's the pay?"

"End of every month. Two dollars and fifteen cents, so long as you haven't lost any papers."

George grinned the entire ride home. More than two whole dollars every month! He began to dream of all the ways he could spend that money. His mouth watered thinking of all the ice cream he could get at Ruska's, the local restaurant. And soda. Crisp, orange, bubbly soda. The end of the month couldn't come fast enough.

♦ ♦ ♦

Not wanting to sit at home in the heat, George began heading east out of town toward Rice Lake. It had been a couple of weeks since they dropped Will off at Old Widower Robinson's, and he wanted to check in. It was a long ride, but at least it gave him something to do for the remainder of the day.

After miles of pedaling, he finally bumped down the dirt path to the clearing where the log cabin sat.

"Will? Hey, Will!" he hollered as he arrived.

"George!" Will came out from the barn, shirtless and wearing a large grin on his face. "You came back!"

"Had to check on you. How's it going?"

"Great, I love it out here! Peaceful, quiet, and this old widower is the best cook I've ever eaten for." Will patted his belly.

"Has he been keeping you busy?" George asked.

"You bet. I've been helping him out real good. Chopped wood, cleaned his chimney, started harvesting some vegetables from his garden, and did all sorts of fishing. He has the best fishing hole in the river down the hill behind his cabin. Got a minute? I'll show you."

George propped his bicycle against the woodshed. Will grabbed two fishing poles from the barn, and they took off down the hill.

They perched on a fallen tree a few feet above the rushing current, bare feet dangling and faces enjoying the sunshine after last week's rain. A soft breeze provided relief from the summer heat.

"Hand me that jar of fish eggs," George said to Will.

George slipped a slimy opaque egg onto his hook and dropped the line into the swift current below. It quickly sank out of sight. He gripped his birch pole tightly in anticipation.

"There's gotta be some monster fish today," said Will. "All this rain should have brought in the big ones."

"They better be hungry," said George.

The boys jigged their poles up and down, waiting impatiently for the telltale *snap* of the line tightening and the subsequent tug in their hands that would indicate a fish had taken their bait.

George looked upstream to the place where small rapids overflowed into the river rushing below their feet. Heavy rains from the week prior had saturated the land, sending swift currents of water downstream.

"Think the water's too fast?" he asked.

"Nah, the bigger the current, the bigger the fish. Just wait. I'll show you how to catch a big one."

The hot afternoon sun baked on the boys as they sat in silence, waiting for a bite. Soon, the breeze died down, and the only bites they were getting were from the black flies that had located the boys and decided they'd make a delicious midday meal.

"Scram! Scram, you nasty flies!" said Will, swatting his hands over his head.

Red welts were already rising on the boys' exposed skin where the flies had begun to snack.

"Forget about the fish. Let's get out of here," said Will.

The boys pulled up their lines, pocketed the bait, slung their fishing poles over their shoulders, and headed for the cabin. Their bare feet marched over a path worn in the earthen floor next to the riverbank, an indication of Will's frequent trips to the fishing spot. Flies buzzed hungrily around their heads, and they swatted them away the best they could while clutching their poles. As soon as the woods gave way to the grassy hill, they began to run.

"You should come fishing with me and John if you can make it into town," George suggested. "We've got a fishing hole up near the dam a bit north of town. We're planning to go on Sunday after church."

"The widower does have a bicycle. It's a rusty old thing, but I can dig it out of the barn and see if he'll let me take it to town." The scrawny boy thought for a minute. "Does that mean I have to come to church?"

"If you do, then you can join us for Sunday dinner. My mother got a ham from our neighbor, Mr. Lindholm."

"Think she'll make me go back to Olson's farm?"

"No, she's been humming and singing like no tomorrow since you ran away. What do you say? There will be plenty of ham."

"I'll be there," said Will, licking his lips in anticipation.

"Great, see you on Sunday. Glad to see you're doing well." George waved as he straddled his bicycle and headed back toward town.

♦ ♦ ♦

The church was within walking distance from George's house, only one block down and half a block over. It was a white two-story building. The main floor was for worship, and the lower level was where church gatherings and meals would occasionally take place. His family always walked to church together, rain or shine, hot or cold. He felt Albert's absence the most on Sundays. The vacancy in the church pew was always noticeable.

But today, that empty spot would be filled. Will was leaning against the brick steps, watching the churchgoers file into the building.

"George!" He leaped up and waved. "Sir, ma'am," he nodded in turn at George's parents.

"Will, what happened to you?" asked George's mother. "Are you all right?"

She eyed the clothes that had once belonged to Albert now covering Will's much smaller frame. George knew there was a level of comfort that she would feel by having a piece of Albert sit with them in church.

"I'm all right," he responded. "Found me a home. You got no need to worry, ma'am. Thank you for all you did for me."

She nodded. George was grateful the church service was about to start and she couldn't push the subject any further.

"I was beginning to wonder if I had come to the wrong church," Will said to George as he climbed the steps with the family.

"How long have you been waiting?"

"Since sunup."

"Since sunup?"

"Didn't want to miss it," said Will with a smile. "A little

church, a lot of ham. Seems like a good bargain to me."

George followed his family into the church as hymns from the pipe organ filled the air. They settled into their usual pew, and in an instant, the heat wave rolled over them. The windows and doors were open, but the lack of breeze meant the effort was futile.

Today's sermon was of the extra-long variety. George's family was one of many from the area whose parents or grandparents had immigrated from Finland. The traditional Sunday sermon was spoken completely in Finnish. But once a month, the minister would first speak the sermon in Finnish, then a second minister would translate to English. The Sunday services with the translated sermons were twice as long, and the attention spans waned quickly for the children, especially in the heat.

"Psst!" Will nudged George's leg.

George knew better than to talk during church, but he looked over at Will. His eyes widened with awe and curiosity. In his hands, Will was holding two green tree frogs and a black salamander.

"Wanna hold one?" he whispered.

George did indeed want to hold one. And he knew holding a small creature in church couldn't be harmful. It was a quiet activity. Plus, the boys were at the end of the pew, far away from George's parents, with eight of his siblings between them.

Will passed one of the tree frogs to George. Its sticky legs clung to his arm. The frog, mistaking George's arm for a new home, climbed higher and higher, nestling into his armpit. The boys couldn't help giggling, which attracted a tap on their shoulders from his oldest sister, Helena.

"Shh!"

The boys stifled their giggles. Will showed George the salamander, nodding for him to take it. George carefully picked up the slimy black amphibian. He was stroking it, marveling over the tiny yellow speckles on its back, when the tree frog decided it didn't like the armpit for a home. It launched into the air, straight into the hair of the old lady who sat directly in front of them.

She flinched, reaching up to see what had hit her. The frog, ever hopeful it had found another new home, latched onto her fingers with its sticky feet. The old lady shrieked and flailed her arm. The frog lost its grip and sailed over three pews before landing at the front of the church.

"My frog!" gasped Will, pocketing his remaining tree frog and grabbing the salamander from George. "I need my frog!"

He slid out of the pew and dashed up the side aisle of the church to retrieve the green frog that was now happily hopping in front of the pulpit.

Quiet pockets of laughter broke out from the congregation as Will dodged this way and that, hunched over as he chased after the leaping frog. The salamander was still tightly clutched in one hand as he stumbled over his own feet. In a brilliant display of acrobatics, he managed to catch the frog in mid-hop before it went behind the pulpit.

The ministers paused their translation, never before having witnessed such an interruption during a sermon.

Will looked up, his face seared red with embarrassment as he turned to face the congregation.

"Sorry," he said meekly, bobbing his head. Then he turned and bolted through the open door at the front of the church, clutching his precious creatures.

◆ ◆ ◆

It was late evening when the boys returned from their day spent fishing. George walked into the barn to put away his fishing pole and saw Taavi leaning over the map on his worktable. George peered over Taavi's shoulder, watching him draw intricate lines across the face of Europe. They had been keeping track of the battles together now for nearly six weeks. The Allied progress was slow but steady. Albert had written home once already, and Taavi's prediction that he would head to northern Africa was accurate. A small stick figure with an *A* over its head was placed in the country of Algeria.

Taavi stood in silence, drawing a circle around the island of Sicily in the Mediterranean Sea, marking the latest Allied victory.

Finally, he spoke. "You helped that orphan boy escape, didn't you?"

George stood still. Taavi's voice was soft, similar to Father's when he was wanting answers.

"Are you going to tell Mother?" George asked, his voice sticking in his throat.

Taavi drew three small arrows toward the bottom of Italy, the part of the country that was shaped like the toe of a boot.

"Not unless you want me to. But if I had to guess, I think Mother was very grateful that she didn't have to send him back to the Olson farm. Where'd he go?"

"We took him to Old Widower Robinson's cabin."

"Well, then, Will is a lucky boy. He'll be happy there." Taavi paused and looked up from the map. "Just don't make a habit out of disobeying Mother."

"Of course not," George said, breathing a sigh of relief that he wasn't going to get in trouble. He helped Taavi roll up the map and nearly skipped out of the barn into the evening sunshine.

7

The Carnival Arrives
August 1943

"They're here, they're here! Come quick!" George's sister, Eva, burst through the back door.

"Who's here? What's here?" Mary asked.

"The carnival is here. Hurry up!"

At her announcement, the children rushed out of the house and clambered through the yard to the end of the block where their road intersected with Pine Street. They looked down the brick road, where a long line of vehicles rattled and bounced into view, heading for the fairgrounds on the opposite end of town.

George stepped into the street to get a better view. Never before had the carnival been this far north. It had always stopped several hours south, too far away for his family to travel.

But this year, the mining company had finally turned its first hefty profit since the Great Depression. They funded the traveling carnival to head farther north to entertain their workers and the subsequent townsfolk.

"George!" his sister Helena scolded. "Get back in the grass. You'll get trampled!"

George took a step back, staring in awe as the large carnival trucks rolled past. The first three trucks were piled high with equipment. Tent poles, canvases, tarps, tools, and ropes burst through the wooden slats of the truck beds.

Following that were several huge rigs, but George couldn't figure out what they were.

"What's that?" George asked Mary.

"Those are the rides. I think that big one is the Ferris wheel. And the one with all the carved animals will be the merry-go-round. I'm not sure about that orange one."

A Ferris wheel! George had only seen a Ferris wheel in the magazines that Mother occasionally got in the mail. He couldn't even imagine what it would feel like to ride around and around, higher than even the tallest pines.

Next was a large bus, longer than any vehicle George had ever seen. It was white, with the words "Grandstand Carnival" painted in bold red letters on the side. People of all ages hung out of the windows, smiling and waving and laughing as they bounced down the bumpy road following the equipment. George waved in return, cheering as the friendly faces rolled past.

"Oh, George, look!" Eva squealed, grabbing his arm and pointing to the next vehicle. "Monkeys!"

Sure enough, almost as if taken straight out of a page in his schoolbook, a trailer with metal bars went by carrying three brown monkeys. They clung to the iron, watching the people on the side of the road as if the entertainment were on the outside of the caged trailer rather than the inside.

"What do you suppose is in that one?" asked George's little brother, Robert, pointing to the next vehicle in line.

The next trailer was windowless, so they couldn't see inside. But on the outside, the words "Grandstand Carnival" were nestled into a painted scene of birds, snakes, lizards, and other small animals.

"I bet that's for the reptiles and small creatures," said Mary. "They could get injured from the sun and wind, so they are kept safely inside."

George stared in awe as the last two trailers drove by. In the first one, two huge golden lions paced back and forth behind the bars. Their eyes darted to and fro as they restlessly watched the growing crowds on the street.

And in the very last trailer, there was an animal larger than George thought possible.

"An elephant," he breathed, staring at the huge creature. It was so big he didn't even know how it could turn around in the trailer.

The line of carnival vehicles slowed to a standstill, and in protest, the larger of the two lions let out a resounding roar. George jumped, covering his ears as a second roar followed.

Slowly, the caravan inched forward and continued toward the fairgrounds to set up for their three-day stay.

"Think we can go to the carnival tomorrow?" he asked wistfully to no one in particular.

"I suppose your father and I couldn't deprive you children of such a special treat," said his mother as she ruffled his hair. She had joined the crowd, taking time away from her mending to watch the carnival come to town. She put an arm around George's shoulder, pulling him close. "We could all use a distraction from the war these days, right, Yrjö?"

♦ ♦ ♦

George could hardly keep his mind on his chores that evening. He could hear the faint music of the carnival as the workers set up the grounds. If he walked to Pine Street, he could see the very top of the Ferris wheel, the colorful, twinkling lights ready for nightfall.

Just as he was hauling in the last of the wood for tomorrow's cooking needs, John came panting around the corner of the barn in the backyard.

"George, come quick! The carnival workers are having a hootenanny. There's music and dancing and the largest bonfire I've ever seen."

George dropped the logs he was carrying into the woodbox just inside the back door and took off after John. The evening sunlight was beginning to fade. He figured they could take a quick peek at the hootenanny and be back before nightfall. They'd be so fast, no one would even notice they were gone.

The boys ran through the woods, using the railroad tracks as a guide to get to the fairgrounds. As they neared the clearing, the hustle and bustle of the carnival greeted them. Heavy machinery sputtered and groaned in the evening air. Generators chugged their rations of gasoline. The large group of carnival workers was circled around the bonfire, a few of them playing lively music. High above the flames, a spit turned slowly. Juicy meat glistened in the firelight.

John motioned for George to follow, and they crept along the edge of the brush around the clearing, getting as close to the bonfire as possible while still staying out of sight.

They watched, hardly blinking, so they wouldn't miss a moment of the action. Carnival workers mingled around the bonfire. They were the most mismatched group of people the boys had ever seen. Babies and old people. Children and adults. Women and men. George could make out one man with a peg leg. Another walked around the fire passing out plates and cups, his hair falling in braids to his shoulders. A man wearing a feathered costume stepped up to the fire, removing the meat from the spit.

The wind shifted directions and drifted straight at the boys huddled in the trees, bringing with it the savory aroma of tender meat. George's mouth watered. Roast. A luxury that his family could never afford. He wondered how the carnival workers were able to get such rations.

George absentmindedly took a step forward to get a better look, not seeing a large fallen tree limb in the dark. He tumbled forward into the firelight, gasping for breath as he fell onto his stomach.

"Oof," he groaned.

"Hey!" shouted one of the carnival workers.

"Run!" yelled John.

But George's foot was tangled up in the tree branch, and before he could take off into the night, strong hands grabbed his arms and held him tight.

"Where'd you come from, son?" a large man asked. "You out here looking to cause trouble tonight?"

"N—no, sir," George stammered, terrified at what the strange carnival workers might do to him.

"What were you doing creeping in the bushes?"

"Just lis—listening to your music, sir. Trying to watch the carnival."

"Well, you don't need to watch us from the dark," he boomed. "All's welcome in the carnival life."

With that, the man helped George up and led him over to the fire. He held his plate out to another man who was carving the roast. George watched as thick, juicy slices of meat piled onto the plate. The man who helped him in the woods plucked up a piece of meat with his fingers and offered it to George.

"Here, have a taste."

George took a savory bite, closing his eyes as the tender meat nearly melted in his mouth. The man fed him another piece of roast. Then another and another. George gobbled them up, never before having tasted such delicious meat.

As he finished his fourth slice of roast, a fiddle started into a new tune, quickly followed by a banjo, a guitar, and some drums. The stars sparkled overhead, and George sat around the bonfire with the carnival workers. He ate two more slices of meat, clapped and tapped along with the music, and occasionally glanced toward the woods with hopes that John would join.

Finally, knowing he had long overstayed his welcome and his

family might soon begin to worry where he was, George said his thanks and slipped back into the night. John was nowhere in sight. George guessed he had long since returned home.

His brothers and sisters were in bed by the time he walked through the back door. Mother and Father were huddled around the radio, the low volume sharing news of the faraway war.

Mother's lips were thin lines as George walked in.

"Where have you been, Yrjö? I've been worried sick that something happened to you."

"I got roast, Mother. Real roast!"

"Roast? Who's giving you roast?"

"The carnival workers. They had roast and music and a huge bonfire."

"Yrjö. You stay away from the carnival workers at night. Lord only knows what kind of riffraff they brought into town. It's no place for a boy to be alone."

George thought back to the man who had helped him up from the woods and treated him to the juicy roast.

"But Mother, they were nice. They offered me food. You always said it's nice to offer food to the hungry. And I was certainly hungry."

A smile tugged at the corners of her mouth. "Ah, yes, George, it is. But I don't want you there alone at night and getting into trouble."

George nodded, promising that he would listen to her warning.

"Can we still go to the carnival tomorrow? They have the

Ferris wheel all set up. It has lights and everything. I know you would love it. You could probably see clear across the ocean to Albert from the top. Can we please go?"

Mother smiled her soft smile. "Of course, we can go. But in the daylight, and with your brothers and sisters—not after hours. Now, head upstairs and get to bed. You'll need all the rest you can get for the fun day ahead."

George washed up, said his prayers, climbed the stairs, and drifted off to sleep with visions of the carnival swirling in his mind.

8

Back to School
September 1943

"Come on, George. Hurry up or you'll be late," Eva hollered as she turned around at the top of the hill.

Best news I've heard all day, George thought as he trudged toward the three-story brick school, his chest filled with dread.

His feet already hurt, and he hadn't even walked the full mile down the cracked town sidewalks. Mother insisted that he had to wear shoes to school, but his feet protested with every step.

Robert ran ahead, catching up with Eva, so he wouldn't be late on the first day of school. But George knew school wasn't going anywhere, whether he was on time or not.

As he pushed the door open to Ms. Johansson's seventh-grade class, he was greeted by the ruckus of nearly thirty students excitedly sharing stories from summer vacation. George made his way to the back of the classroom, claiming a desk that had a perfect view of the football field and running track. The only good thing about seventh grade was that the classroom was on the third floor, so he would have a much easier time daydreaming.

"Mornin', Vulture. I see you managed to scrounge up some shoes."

George groaned inwardly and looked up to see the town bully,

Ricky McClain, leering at him. Ricky had taunted him earlier in the summer on the day the orphan train arrived, teasing George about his family being poor.

"Go away, Ricky," said George, trying to sound as uninterested as possible. He clenched his fists under his desk, wishing Ricky would just leave him alone.

"Any news on your brother yet? He didn't, you know, *die* already, did he?" Ricky snickered. "My father says they put the poor soldiers closer to the front lines. They're more *disposable,* if you know what I mean."

"Shut up, Ricky. Shut up!" George stood at his desk, fists clenched. He had grown over the summer and was now a good four inches taller than Ricky.

Before either of the boys could say another word, the door opened, and Ms. Johansson bustled into the room.

"Sorry to keep you waiting," she said as she walked to the front of the room. Then she glanced toward the back corner. "Boys? What's going on?"

"Nothing, ma'am," said George. "Ricky was just going to find his desk." He kept his eyes on Ricky, watching as he slunk back to his desk on the other side of the classroom.

"Well, I'm glad you've already become acquainted with one another. I know we are going to have a wonderful year."

One by one, she called out the names of the students. Most George knew. But there were some he did not. The jobs in the copper mines brought families from near and far to the town, so every year there was an influx of new children starting school. And at the end of each year, it was inevitable that some would leave town and never return. The mines paid well, but they were dangerous, and not everyone could handle the work. Besides, if someone got injured—or, worse yet, killed—those families almost always left town in search of a new line of work or to return to where they came from.

Ms. Johansson finished with attendance and called the class to attention.

"As you all know, we are still taking precautions for the war concerning the safety of our students. Since we are on the third floor of this building, it is very important to be prepared in case of an air raid. Therefore, let us practice taking cover."

She motioned for the children to assume their positions. George pushed his chair back and crawled under his desk. He pulled himself into the smallest ball possible, protecting his head and neck with his hands. It wasn't as easy this year as it had been last year. His increased height caused him to get very uncomfortable very fast. He breathed a sigh of relief when Ms. Johansson called the drill to a close and told them to sit in their chairs.

"Now, just remember," she said, "we will be practicing air raid drills during the year. As soon as you hear the sirens, you are to take cover."

The rest of the morning passed quickly enough. Ms. Johansson passed out their schoolbooks, pencils, and a notebook of blank paper that would soon enough be filled with equations, spelling words, geography lessons, and personalized scribbles from each student.

Finally, the bell rang, dismissing the students for their hour-and-fifteen-minute lunch break. George sprang from his desk, scrambled down the two flights of stairs, took the shortcut across the football field, and skittered into the kitchen at home in no time.

"Goodness, Yrjö," his mother exclaimed. "You must be starving, to come busting through the door so quickly. Here, I made some sandwiches. Where are your sisters and brother?"

George hadn't seen Robert, Eva, Mary, or Catherine since they set out earlier in the morning.

"Don't know, but Mother, can we please listen to the noontime war program?" he asked, hoping she wouldn't mind switching the station from her Modern Woman program.

"I suppose, but what's got your worries rising?"

George wasn't going to tell her about Ricky's taunts, but he had to admit to himself that it did refresh his worries about Albert.

Every day at noon, the five-minute war update came on the radio. During the summer, George had often missed the noon update, as he was busy fishing or playing with friends. But during the school year, it was the perfect lunchtime news program.

George was halfway through his second sandwich when his siblings came chattering animatedly through the door. Together, they listened to the war news, finished their lunch, and finally began their walk back to school for the remainder of the afternoon lessons.

♦ ♦ ♦

The afternoon was hot and sticky. The early September sun was still quite warm. After his lessons for the day were complete, George walked out into the warm sunshine, calling for John as he walked across the courtyard.

"Did you see Will today?" John asked.

"No. Do you think Old Widower Robinson would make him come to school?" George asked.

"It'd be a far walk or bicycle ride to do every day. And the widower doesn't have an automobile."

"Lucky Will. I wish I lived too far away to go to school."

The boys walked in silence down the sidewalk toward home. They dreamed of a day when they wouldn't be confined to the four walls of a classroom and could instead roam the wilderness all day.

As they walked across the football field, George parted ways with John and took a detour to *The Suomi Times* printshop. It was the first Tuesday of September, so he wanted to see if his boss had his payment ready from the August deliveries.

"See you later," he waved to John.

He cut across the town park to the printshop on Fifth Street.

"Hello, Gurney? You in there?" George nudged the back door open. He could smell Gurney's musky tobacco smoke mixed with warm ink and paper.

"George, come on in, son! I was beginning to wonder if you forgot about payday," the elderly shop owner said with a smile.

His lit pipe dangled from his lips, bouncing ever so slightly as he spoke.

"School started today," George explained his tardiness in coming to collect his money. His heart was beating fast, excitement building as he imagined all the cold ice cream and soda he'd soon be able to purchase.

Gurney disappeared into his office for a moment, returning with a handful of coins for George.

"Here you go. Not quite a full month of pay since you started mid-month, but you've earned every penny. Run along now, and don't spend it all in one afternoon," Gurney chuckled as George ran down the back steps.

George had dreamed of this moment since he began his paper route. Every Tuesday and Thursday for the past few weeks, he had spent several hours walking the neighborhoods. He braved the weather, did his best to keep stray dogs at bay, and flung newspaper after newspaper onto front porches and walkways.

He stopped in front of Ruska's, pulling the handful of coins from his pocket. He counted it out. One dollar and seventy-five cents. Never had he earned so much money at one time. Scrap metal paid pennies. Even the odd chores he did for his elderly neighbor, Mr. Lindholm, or Aunt Elvie, who lived on the other side of Pine Street, usually just yielded a nickel here, a nickel there, and a dime on a very lucky day.

His mouth watered. He could almost taste the sweet vanilla ice cream. He'd even ask for chocolate fudge topping. And soda. Orange flavored. Crisp, bubbly orange soda. Maybe root beer. He couldn't decide which flavor he wanted and figured he would just buy both since he had enough money.

Just as he was about to push the door open, he pictured Mother bent over her sewing table, working late into the night. Lately, it seemed she never said no to any mending orders that came her way. And George knew why. Winter was coming, and all the children had grown like weeds over the summer. Boots and jackets were expensive, even though they shopped at Cheap Joe's, the secondhand store on Third Avenue.

George looked longingly through the window, then turned and walked the rest of the way home with the dollar seventy-five secured deep in his pocket.

"Here, Mother. For you," George said as he held out his hands and showed her the coins.

"Why, whatever is this, George?"

"From my newspaper route. But I want you to have it."

"Oh," his mother cried out, "*kiitos,* Yrjö." *Thank you,* George. "You are too kind."

"It's so you don't have to stay up so late doing all that sewing."

"Ah, but it's a labor of love that I do it, *rakas poika.*" *Dear boy.* "I do the work so my children can be taken care of. You know that. I don't mind one bit."

"I know, but maybe it can help a little."

"Of course, it will. It will certainly help. Thank you, George." She kissed his hair. "Now, you take at least two of these coins and make sure you get yourself a treat. You've certainly earned it."

His mother pressed a five- and ten-cent piece into his hands and deposited the rest of the coins into the tin can in the bedroom.

George grinned as he raced out of the house and down the street toward Ruska's, ready to spend some of his fifteen cents on a delicious, sugary treat.

9

Victorious Garden
September 1943

"George, come here, please," Mother called from the back steps. Her hair was tied up and covered by a piece of plaid cloth, forehead damp with sweat.

George wiped his dirty hands on his pant legs, glad he was assigned to picking the vegetables from the garden instead of in the hot kitchen where the canning process was underway.

"Yes, Mother?"

"Can you please run to Jenkins's store and pick up some supplies? I'm all out of cheesecloth and need four dozen more canning lids."

"Be right back," he said, and headed down Pine Street.

"Hello, George," the friendly grocer welcomed him into the dim store.

It took a moment for George's eyes to adjust to the sunlight streaming in through the windows on either side of the door, but once they did, he looked at the shelves and barrels of goods behind the tall counter where the grocer stood.

"'Morning, Mr. Jenkins," George said as he walked across the creaking wooden floorboards.

"What brings you in today?"

"Mother needs cheesecloth and lids. Four dozen lids."

"Harvest time, I take it?"

"Yes, sir. We finished the beans, carrots, cucumbers, and peas last weekend. Hopefully, we can get the rest in before dark—except for the pumpkins, squash, and apples."

"Looks like the weather should hold out. What are you bringing in today?" the grocer asked as he placed the requested goods on the counter.

"Beets, corn, tomatoes, onions, and potatoes. Lots and lots of potatoes." George looked down at his fingers, the residue of the potato harvest caked in layers of dirt on his hands and under his fingernails.

"Good luck," Mr. Jenkins said as he pushed the cheesecloth and lids across the counter. "Tell your mother I've put this on her tab. She can pay at the end of the month as usual."

George thanked him and walked home with the supplies in hand. He entered the hot kitchen where every surface and corner of the room was overflowing with jars, vegetables, canning supplies, sisters, and cookware.

"George is back," Ann called out, taking the supplies from him. "*Kiitos.*"

"Back outside for you, young man," Mother said, squeezing his shoulders and shooing him out the door.

The cool autumn breeze was a welcome relief on his face as he walked back to the garden.

"Grab these baskets," Taavi called from the middle of the potato patch. His pants were completely soiled from the dirt, and he was surrounded by mounds of freshly dug potatoes.

Overflowing bushel baskets of potatoes were lined up at the edge of the garden waiting to be taken inside. One by one, George hauled them inside and down the steep steps to the cellar. Father was busy spreading the potatoes in large, shallow, stacked bins. The cool cellar air would help the potato skins harden just enough to heal any blemishes, keep the bugs out, and prevent them from rotting. It would take two weeks for them to fully cure. Once cured, the potatoes would be transferred to barrels layered with sawdust to keep them protected from cold and moisture. The family would then be able to enjoy fresh potatoes all winter long.

George made trip after trip up and down the stairs, bringing basket upon basket of potatoes into the cellar.

"Thank you, George," his father said as he made one final trip into the dark underground room and deposited the last bushel basket onto the dirt floor.

George's arms were weak and his back ached, but he knew the hard work was necessary. Without a harvest, they would go hungry all winter long.

He thought back to just a few winters ago when food and money were still scarce during the Great Depression. He remembered the familiar pangs of hunger in his belly. The nights spent lying awake as his body ached for food. Meals were once a day—twice if they were lucky—and meager at best. Thankfully, the soup lines provided food for those in need, but even then, it was never enough.

But with such a bountiful harvest and the war providing jobs and money, he knew this winter would be one of relative plenty. Once the potatoes were safely tucked inside the cellar, George went back outside into the bright autumn sunshine.

"Can you help with the corn?" his little brother, Robert, asked. "Please?"

George looked at the mountain of corn piled around Robert and sat down on the grass to help him shuck the yellow cobs free of their green husks.

"This is going to take forever," Robert whispered.

George nodded in agreement. They knew they shouldn't complain about the harvest chores, but the days spent in the garden were long and tiring.

"I know, but maybe if we finish early enough, we'll be able to go swimming at the dam."

The boys knew they'd need a good scrubbing in the water after the harvest chores were done, and it was more fun to clean up at the swimming hole than the washroom at home.

Father soon emerged from the cellar and began to help the boys with the corn. By late afternoon, with help from the entire family, the harvest was complete for the day. The corn was shucked, the beets and onions were pulled from the garden, and the tomatoes were carefully removed from their vines and brought inside for Mother and the sisters to preserve.

George went into the kitchen and watched for a few moments. The busy hustle and bustle of the canning process was always a welcome sight. The smell of vinegar, salt, garlic, and pepper mixed with other aromatic spices filled the air and tickled his nose.

"Don't just stand there," Mary ordered. "Help us bring these downstairs." She motioned to the long rows of glass jars that covered the kitchen table.

Armful by careful armful, George helped bring the jars filled with colorful vegetables to the cellar. Once done, he stood back to admire their hard work. The shelves were filled with vibrant hues, and he knew there were still some corners of the cellar that needed to be filled. The pumpkins, squash, and apples would come in at the end of the month. And Taavi was certain to get a deer or two in the fall. Then, they would be all set for the cold winter ahead.

♦ ♦ ♦

"Ready?" Taavi asked as the last of the canning supplies were put away for the day.

"I've got the soap and towels," George said. "Robert is waiting outside."

The three boys headed toward the dam behind their house. The early evening light cast long shadows across the trail through the woods. During the warm summer months, they went to the swimming hole almost daily. Now that the weather was getting colder, it was probably one of their last times going swimming for the year.

They left their clothes in a pile on the grassy bank. George dove in headfirst, staying underwater as long as his lungs would allow. The water was crisp and refreshing. It soothed the aching blisters on his hands and calmed the pain in his back. He popped up, splashing water on his face and rubbing his hands to clean the dirt that was embedded into his skin.

"Don't forget to scrub with soap," Taavi said as he passed the lavender-scented bar to George.

The boys scrubbed until their hair and skin were clean, getting the worst part of their outdoor bath out of the way first so they could then focus on having fun.

They had breath-holding contests, underwater swimming races, and rode the rope swing that flung them far out into the water.

"I wish Albert were here to teach us how to backflip off the swing. He never did get to teach us that before he left," Robert said.

"You'll have to wait until he gets back," Taavi laughed. "I'm not risking my neck like he would to teach you any tricks."

The boys all looked longingly at the swing. Albert was always the one doing the wildest stunts on it. He could flip and twist into the water better than anyone else in town.

"It would have been nice to have him help haul all of those vegetables today," said Taavi.

"And he's the best checkers player, too," said George. "I wish the war wasn't so far away."

"I wish he could just come home," whispered Robert.

"Soon enough, he will," Taavi reassured his younger brothers. "Maybe tonight we can listen to the radio and see if we can mark any more victories on the map. Now that Italy has surrendered to the Allies, maybe our boys can start pushing the Germans out. And don't worry about Albert. I'm sure he'll be back in no time. Now, let's dry off and head home for supper. I don't know about you, but I'm starving."

George's stomach rumbled in agreement. But as they walked through the woods toward home, he wished he could be just as certain that Albert would come home soon.

10

Potato Harvest
September 1943

Even though it was a Monday morning, George skipped down the stairs. He was grinning from ear to ear and couldn't wait to start the day. This year, being as he was now twelve, he was old enough to partake in the potato harvest in the valley just outside of town. All the children who were of age and whose parents allowed it were released from school during the harvest. Without their help, the farmers would never be able to get their entire crop out of the fields before the weather turned cold.

"I hope it's a huge harvest this year," George said, hopping from one foot to the other as he and Eva pulled on their shoes and an extra layer of warm clothing.

"I want to go!" Robert sulked, upset that he was going to be the only sibling walking to school all week.

"I just hope there are enough workers, so it goes quickly. I don't want to miss too much school," said Mary.

"Hopefully, it's so big that we can miss school all week," countered George. "And maybe next week, too."

Mary rolled her eyes, but Eva agreed with George. She would also rather be outside instead of cooped up in a stuffy classroom.

Just before eight o'clock, George, Eva, Mary, and Catherine

walked to the town square to hitch a ride to the valley. They climbed into the bed of a rusty black pickup truck with a dozen other children, ready for a day of hard work.

"I heard we're at the Smith farm this year," Eva whispered to George as they bumped down the road. "I'm glad, because he pays five cents a bushel. If we work fast, we can each make at least two dollars per day. By the end of the week, together we'll have at least forty dollars!"

Forty dollars! George couldn't even imagine that amount of money. It was more than he'd ever seen in his entire life.

The truck dropped the children off at the east end of Mr. Smith's potato field. Inside the red barn were stacks and stacks of wooden bushel baskets. One of Mr. Smith's hired hands was there, handing out pitchforks and giving instructions. George followed Eva's lead by grabbing a pitchfork, a stack of bushel baskets, and heading into the field.

All morning long, they dug potatoes from the soft brown dirt. They had to dig fast enough to fill their baskets efficiently but not too fast that they pierced the delicate skin of the potatoes with their pitchforks. A broken potato would quickly rot, ruining the rest that it was packaged with.

They stopped at lunchtime for a break, eating the ham and cheese sandwiches that Mother had sent in a tin pail.

"Doing okay?" Catherine asked George.

He nodded, mouth full. His hands were blistered. His back ached. And they had acres and acres of potatoes still left to dig up. But he was determined to get through the entire harvest without a single complaint. He felt a sense of pride in being able to help his family with the finances. Extra money meant life would be easier and more comfortable for everyone in the house.

♦ ♦ ♦

Throughout the remainder of the week, George pulled dirty potatoes from the rich soil and put them into baskets. It seemed as if potatoes had taken over his life. He woke up thinking about potatoes. He dug potatoes all day while the sun shone brightly overhead. He went home in the bed of the pickup truck thinking about potatoes. He even dreamed of potatoes when his weary body lay down on his mattress at night.

Finally, shortly after lunch on Friday afternoon, the last bushel basket full of potatoes was brought to the red barn and tallied in the ledger by Mr. Smith's hired hand. The children stood in line to receive a paper ticket that showed how many bushel baskets of potatoes they had harvested, so they could be paid accordingly.

George took his ticket, proud of the hard work that he had done over the past five days.

"How many did you get?" Eva asked, eyes bright with excitement.

"Two hundred and twenty-five," George beamed, glancing down at his yellow slip of paper.

"Good job, Yrjö! Mother will be proud of that, especially for your first time."

"How many did you get?"

"Two hundred and sixty. Come on, let's go see what Mary and Catherine got."

They walked across the barn to their older sisters, who were talking to their friends.

"How many did you get this year?" Eva asked the girls.

"Two ninety," said Mary.

"I got three oh five," Catherine beamed, proud to have been able to crack three hundred bushels—her personal best.

The children were rounded up and then sat in the bed of the pickup truck for one last ride back to town, their destination the local bank. The teller would pay each child their earnings and deduct it from the corresponding farmer's bank account that was listed on their yellow slip of paper.

The bank was a noisy spectacle. George guessed there were close to one hundred children receiving their potato harvest pay. Each one was talking animatedly, grinning from ear to ear at their good fortune.

"Hey! Hey, George," he heard a familiar voice through the crowd.

"Will! How are you?" George greeted his orphan friend.

"Better than ever. Just got done harvesting Mr. Jacobson's field."

"How many bushels did you get?" George asked.

"Two hundred and twenty-five," Will said proudly.

"Same here," George laughed, showing his friend the yellow ticket printed with black ink.

The boys chatted for a few moments before stepping in line to collect their money from the teller. She smiled as she handed George his earnings, congratulating him on a harvest well done.

George said goodbye to Will, then raced home with his sisters. They rushed into the kitchen, each one trying to talk over the other as they told Mother all about the potato harvest. They put their money in a stack on the table.

"Here, Mother," Mary said as she pushed the stack across the table. "Fifty-four dollars."

Mother smiled her sweet smile.

"Ah, what did I do to deserve such sweet children?" she asked, hugging each one and kissing them on top of their heads. "You are all so kind, but you must remember to take your portion of the harvest earnings to spend as you please."

And even though the children protested, telling her that she should keep all the money, she took four one-dollar bills from the pile and handed one to each child.

George sat at the table, smoothing out the dollar. He had never had a bill before. Some coins here and there, but never a whole one-dollar bill. He didn't even know what to spend it on, so he decided to tuck it away in his dresser drawer. He wanted to keep it crisp and clean until the time came when he knew what to buy. He ran upstairs and carefully tucked it into his sock that still held a leftover nickel from his paper route earnings.

George's father entered the house as Mary and Eva were setting the table for supper.

"Here's a letter for you, Aina," he said, handing a small white envelope to George's mother.

"What is it?" George asked.

His mother read the script on the outside of the envelope. "It's from Finland," she said, her voice almost a whisper. "It looks like my mother's writing—your grandmother."

She set the letter on the counter, telling the children to come and eat.

"But can't we read it now?" Catherine asked.

"We'll read it after supper, when Taavi is home. A letter from Finland is a special treat, and we don't want anyone to miss out."

The sun had already set by the time the supper dishes were washed and put away. The evening chores had been completed. George was setting up the checkerboard on the kitchen table so he and Robert could play. Finally, Taavi returned from his workday in the copper mines, and the family gathered in the living room to hear the news from across the Atlantic Ocean.

My dearest Aina, the letter began, *I hope this letter finds you, Solomon, and the children well.*

Mother's sweet voice filled the room, sharing the news from Finland.

The German army remains in the northern region of Lapland. It is a difficult situation for everyone. Without Germany, we would have even less food and fuel than the meager amounts we have now. But even with the Germans sending food to our markets, we are still hungry. Oh, some days it seems we cannot possibly make it until another morning.

The Germans have also been helping us keep the Soviets from invading our entire country, as our small army can only do so much against Stalin's mighty Red Army. Our boys have done their best, but war supplies and weapons would have run out long ago without Germany's help.

Thankfully, they haven't taken over our government—just our land. We are grateful for that, as we have heard whispers of the horrible things happening in mainland Europe, where they've been rounding up the Jews and sending them away. I pray that doesn't happen here.

We await the day when the Germans leave, and Finland can return to the land of peace we once knew. Though I'm sure they will not leave easily, as they have taken over our nickel mines in Lapland, which are providing materials for their weapons.

But on the bright side, Olga had her baby girl over the summer, a sweet little Isabel. She's an absolute angel and such a breath of new life during these dark days of death. I hope this letter makes it across the Atlantic.

With all my love,

Äiti.

Mother wiped tears from her eyes and gently folded the letter back to its compact state.

"I wonder what it's like having Germans living a stone's throw from your front door," mused Robert.

"I pray we never find out," said Mother, ruffling his hair.

"Do you really think they are that hungry?" Helena asked.

"Yes, dear, I do believe they are. Your grandmother is a strong woman. She wouldn't share ill news unless it was absolutely dire."

"Can we send them something?" asked Ann. "Food or money?"

"Yes, that is a wonderful idea. We will send a package with

what we can spare. It won't be much, and I hesitate to send money overseas, but let's gather a few things. We must do what we can to help."

Mother placed a cardboard box on the table and began rummaging through the nonperishables in the pantry. In it, she put venison jerky, peanuts, dried berries, and packets of vegetable seeds for George's grandmother to plant in her garden, come springtime. And for the baby, Mother added some tiny, warm clothes that George and his siblings had worn years ago.

In an envelope, Mother took the time to write a letter and placed ten dollars inside. George knew she would send more if she was certain the money would get there. But with the unreliable censorship by military personnel that reviewed all incoming and outgoing mail in both America and Finland, she couldn't risk sending more.

11

The Long Winter Ahead
October 1943

"Drop it there, O'Malley!" Father shouted from where he stood near the woodpile. The large, flatbed delivery truck hissed as the driver shifted it into park.

The driver, Pat O'Malley from the railroad yard, hopped out of the truck to winch up the bed. He wore tall rubber boots and was covered from head to toe in soot and grease.

As he cranked the handle, the truck bed rose to a steeper incline, and the wooden railroad ties tumbled out. One after another, the long timbers fell, until a tangled pile of wood lay in the yard.

"That's good," Father yelled again as the last timber crashed to the ground.

Mr. O'Malley reversed the crank, and the truck bed settled back to its horizontal position.

"You're all set for winter now, Solomon." Mr. O'Malley tipped his hat and climbed back into the truck.

"Thanks again, sir."

"No problem. If you need more, just give a holler. You know where to find me."

The truck sputtered a short protest before roaring back to life.

Then, it bumped down the road, leaving George and his father standing beside the soaring mountain of railroad ties.

"Well, this ought to keep us busy for a while." George's father wiped his brow. "We best tackle what we can this morning. A small dent in the pile is better than no dent at all. Do you want to saw or chop today?"

"I'll chop," George said, though both chores were equally miserable.

George worked next to his father all morning. The chilly, mid-October air reminded them that the railroad ties needed to be cut and split so they would have enough wood to heat the house all winter long. There was a coal stove in the cellar, but coal was expensive, so they used the free wood from the railroad yard as much as they could.

"I'm glad O'Malley was able to get us this load. He might have one more for us in a week or two," said Father.

"That's a lot of chopping," George said, not outwardly complaining, just stating the reality of the situation.

"Yes, but we need to be grateful that we can get so much fuel for no cost. The equivalent amount of coal would cost a small fortune, and thanks to O'Malley's generosity, we get to save that money for something else we need."

George nodded and grabbed the ax, ready to tackle the seemingly unending task of turning the railroad ties into usable firewood. First, Father would remove any railroad spikes that had been accidentally left in the wood. Then, he would use the saw to cut each railroad tie into eight sections, each about twelve inches in length. Lastly, George would use the ax to split the sections into quarters so they would burn easier.

Mr. O'Malley dropped the railroad ties off every fall. They were heavy, rectangular pieces of lumber that sat on the ground and held the metal train tracks in place. The ties and tracks were always in need of maintenance and repair, and when the railroad ties were replaced, the used ones were discarded at the railroad yard. They were covered in soot and grease from the trains, often bent crooked, useless in any capacity other than burning. Even then, they always gave off a pungent odor that stung George's nose whenever he opened the stove door to stoke it with more wood.

But he knew better than to complain. Wood meant heat. And he would gladly smell a little railway residue instead of being cold all winter long.

"Pies are done!" Catherine called from the back steps.

George's stomach rumbled. His arms ached. The ax handle had rubbed blisters into his palms, even though he was wearing gloves. He had long ago lost count of how many railroad ties he had split.

"Let's go eat lunch," said Father, wiping his brow and taking a swig from the water jug at the base of the woodpile. "And after, would you like to come to town with me to visit the harvest market?"

"Yes!" George said with excitement, momentarily forgetting about his aches and pains. He hadn't realized it was already time for the annual harvest market.

As they walked through the back door to wash up, they were greeted by the warm aroma of apples and cinnamon. The apple harvest had been brought in over the past week, and now, his mother and sisters were spending the day preserving the apples to add to the collection of food in the cellar. There was applesauce, apple butter, canned apple slices, and four fresh apple pies.

"Mmm," said George as he bit into a warm piece of apple pie after lunch. "Delicious! Best pie I've ever had."

"You say that about every apple pie you eat," Mother teased with a smile.

"Each one is better than the last," George said, filling his mouth with bite after bite of the sweet dessert.

"We're going to the harvest market for a bit, Aina," George's father told his mother. "Would you like to come with us?"

"I really can't right now. I have to finish this batch of apple butter. But if you find some wool for winter clothes, I could use a few yards for winter dresses for the girls."

♦ ♦ ♦

George trailed half a step behind his father as they weaved in and out of the booths set up in the town square. Vendors were selling every good imaginable—vegetables, fruit, pickled preserves, jams, honey, braided rugs, soap, wooden toys, clothing, and more. The harvest market had something for everyone. It was a lively event. The street was filled with townsfolk milling about as they looked at the merchandise on display.

George's father stopped in front of a crowded booth and George bumped into his legs. He had been paying too much attention to the booths to be watching Father's step. A group of well-dressed ladies surrounded the tables and racks, admiring the fine selection of fur pelts on display.

"Margaret, look at this one. Mink! I've never seen such a fine mink pelt in all my life," a tall, middle-aged woman said.

"Yes, but look at that white rabbit fur. Bright as a fresh snowfall, and you know it would make the warmest pair of mittens," her friend replied.

"You're responsible for these furs, young man?" one of the women asked.

"Yes, ma'am," said the voice.

George knew that voice anywhere. He tugged on his father's coat, pulling him around the group of ladies.

"Will," George said, greeting his friend, "what are you doing here?"

"Good afternoon, sir," Will first addressed George's father, then faced George. "I'm here selling my furs. Old Man Robinson is a fine teacher. Got me my own trap line down by the river. I got a mighty fine collection so far." He puffed his chest out and motioned to the display in his booth.

"I'll say," said George, running his fingers over the softest and thickest fox pelt he had ever seen.

He looked around. The booth was filled with a variety of furs. Beaver, rabbit, fox, mink, otter, and even one wolf pelt and two large bear furs. There was a small fortune of furs displayed at the booth. George knew he could never afford something so luxurious, though the furs would make a toasty pair of mittens for wintertime. He was comforted to see Will doing so well. It meant things were good for him at Old Widower Robinson's cabin. Will was clean, dressed in properly fitting clothes, and had a knife strapped to a sheath on his hip.

"There he is," a shrill voice cut through the brisk, afternoon air. "I told you, that's the boy. Right there, over there."

The crowd in front of Will's booth jostled and then parted down the middle.

"See, that's the one! He's ours. We took him in when no one else wanted him."

Will's face went as white as a sheet, and his eyes clouded over with fear. It was Mr. Olson and his wife. George hadn't seen them since the day the orphan train brought Will to town.

"You're right, Eleanor. That is the boy," Mr. Olson boomed as he put his hands on his wife's shoulders, then stepped closer to Will. Only a few inches separated their faces. "Son, you come back to my house right this instant, or I'll fix you a good one," he threatened.

Mr. Olson's meaty paws grabbed Will's arm, wrenching him close. Will squirmed in protest, but his small frame was no match for the power of Mr. Olson.

"No!" Will protested, panic rising in his voice. "I'm not going back. I don't want to."

"I don't care what you want. You're my son. We paid good money for you. Now, you better march back to my automobile, and then I'll show you where you belong."

George sidestepped the stunned crowd, positioning himself in front of Mr. Olson and Will.

"No," George said, his voice strong even though inside he was terrified. "Will is not yours. He belongs to Mr. Robinson now."

Mr. Olson stared at George. His beady little eyes narrowed to just slits. "What did you say, boy?"

"Will isn't yours. He doesn't belong to you. Let him go." George's voice quivered ever so slightly, but he wasn't about to let his friend go back to Mr. and Mrs. Olson's farm.

Mr. Olson bent down so his eyes were level with George's. He cursed loudly and spat onto the ground at George's feet. "Whose boy are you?" he demanded.

George flinched, recoiling in shock, as he had never been cursed at before.

"Oliver." The strong, steady voice came from behind George. It was Father, using Mr. Olson's first name. "Let him go. The boy isn't yours anymore."

The two men stared at each other for what felt like half of eternity.

Finally, with hatred spewing from his eyes, Mr. Olson released his grip on Will's arm and retreated back into the crowd. His wife continued screeching as they returned to their shiny black automobile, chastising Mr. Olson for giving up.

"Thank you, sir. Oh, thank you, thank you," Will said over and over again as he flung his arms around Father's waist.

"Don't mention it," George's father replied, patting Will on the head. "I'd do it for anyone. No one deserves to be treated so horribly by that man. I wouldn't even give him a stray dog to take care of, let alone a fine lad like yourself."

They stood back and watched as Mr. Olson's automobile squealed out of sight.

♦ ♦ ♦

That evening, as George's family was finishing supper, a knock at the back door alerted them to an unexpected visitor. George's mother opened the door to find Will, arms laden with furs.

"Here you go, ma'am. A small token of thanks for your husband's kindness today." He held out a red fox fur and two white rabbit pelts.

"Why, whatever is this? We cannot take your furs, Will," she said, her mouth agape. "And I'm sorry, but I don't have the money to buy them."

"Your mister saved my life today. It's not much, but it's the least I can do. Thanks again."

And before she could protest any further, Will pushed the fur pelts into her arms and ducked out into the dim evening light.

George smiled as his friend disappeared. Will would go to bed happy tonight, safe once again from Mr. Olson.

12

Albert Writes Home
October 1943

"Helena, hurry up." George banged on the washroom door.

"Mr. Tinney is scheduled to deliver eggs today," Eva snickered. "She's going to be a while."

"Hush! I'm almost done," came the muffled response from the other side of the door.

Helena always got flustered when Mr. Tinney brought his delivery of eggs every Saturday morning. She did her best to capture the young bachelor's attention, and the family always laughed because it seemed to be working. Mr. Tinney always stuck around longer than necessary when he dropped off the eggs and Helena was home.

George also liked when Mr. Tinney brought the eggs, but for entirely different reasons. Mr. Tinney lived down in the valley. Along with his chicken farm, he had a large apple orchard, and he always brought an apple or sweet treat for the younger children, including George.

When a knock echoed on the back door, everyone scrambled to be the first to open it.

Helena bustled out of the washroom, curls bouncing as she hurried to the door to greet Mr. Tinney.

George got to the door first and opened it to find someone who was definitely not Mr. Tinney. He was much shorter and much younger. He had a broad grin plastered on his face and was holding a crate of eggs in his arms.

"Will!" George cried out. "What are you doing here?"

"He's my newest assistant," Mr. Tinney said, walking around the corner of the house with another crate of eggs.

"Assistant? What do you mean?" George asked.

Will beamed. "Old Man Robinson said Tinney needed help with the eggs."

"That's right," Mr. Tinney nodded. "I received a note from Uncle Sam calling me away to other duties for a while. Will is going to keep up on the egg delivery for me until I can return."

"Oh, no!" gasped Helena. "You got a draft card?"

"I most certainly did, miss," he said. "Fresh out of the post the other week. I leave on the noon train, three weeks from today. I meant to come and tell you earlier, but it just never felt like the right time to spring such news on you."

"What's all this talk of draft cards?" asked Mother, coming to join the commotion at the back door. She had a dish towel flung over one shoulder, and worry lined her face.

"Just that, ma'am. Don't know when I'll be back, but Will is going to take good care of you. He's looking after the hens, and I suspect there'll be no shortage of eggs. He's a quick learner and has a knack for animals. And he's tall enough to drive my truck. As long as he's careful and stays out of trouble, the sheriff won't have any reason to give him a second glance. We're mighty short on deliverymen in this town ever since the draft started shipping all of us overseas. There's no room to complain about who delivers the eggs, as long as they're competent. And I know Will is just that."

Mr. Tinney handed the eggs to Helena and patted Will on the shoulder. Will beamed with pride.

"He's going to teach me how to drive his rig this afternoon," Will whispered to George, motioning to the street where Mr. Tinney's old flatbed truck was parked.

George grinned at Will, imagining the freedom a delivery truck would give.

"Maybe you could drive to school this winter," George said, voice filled with hope. Having Will in school would certainly dampen the monotony of the long days spent in the classroom.

"Maybe," said Will, contemplating. "But the trapping is so good this time of year. Besides, I'll have to be careful with the gas rations. I'd hate to have to haul all of these eggs on foot. It's a long uphill walk from the valley to town."

"You'll at least have to come to the Pine Street ice rink once it's ready."

"Now, that is somewhere I can promise to be," Will smiled.

George could hardly wait for the days and nights to get cold enough for the ice rink to be built. He dreamed of evenings after school spent sliding on the ice and watching the hockey games. Someday, he would be able to buy a pair of ice skates so he could play in a real hockey game. But right now, there wasn't enough extra money, so he would continue to slide on his boots over the slippery ice.

"Thank you, Mr. Tinney." Mother was talking to the deliveryman again. "We will be waiting for you to return home, safe and sound."

Mr. Tinney nodded. "Thank you, ma'am. I aim to do just that."

"Goodbye, Mr. Tinney," Helena called, her voice quivering ever so slightly as she waved.

"I'll be back in no time, folks." He handed everyone a honey stick, then returned to his delivery truck with Will in tow.

"Bye, Mr. Tinney," a chorus of voices called from the back steps as they watched him go. "Be safe! Say hello to Albert if you run into him!"

Mr. Tinney gave one last wave as he climbed up into his truck.

George watched longingly as the truck rolled down the street to the next house on the delivery route. Will was the luckiest boy around. Not many twelve-year-old boys got to drive. George hoped Will could teach him how to drive Mr. Tinney's truck before the war was over and Mr. Tinney came home.

♦ ♦ ♦

After lunch, George rode his bicycle over the brick streets to the post office. Mother had tasked him with the important chore of checking the mail.

"Good afternoon, young man," the postmaster greeted

George. "I was hoping someone from your house would make it down here today. This one just arrived yesterday. I reckon you won't want to wait to open it."

George tucked the envelope under his arm and pedaled home as fast as he could. He was out of breath by the time he parked his bicycle in the barn and ran inside.

"Mother! Mother! We got mail from Albert! It's here, right here!"

He waved the envelope in the air as the family clambered around to see.

"Oh, my," Mother breathed, carefully holding the envelope and inspecting the small, black writing. Letters from Albert were few and far between, and always treasured.

"Can we open it? Please?" George begged, unable to wait another moment. He wanted to hear the contents of the letter in hopes that he would be able to figure out where Albert was so he could update the map on Taavi's workbench.

"I'm afraid we will have to wait until your Father and Taavi return. We'll read it together as soon as they get back."

The afternoon dragged on as George waited for Father and Taavi to come home. Finally, after many long hours, the back door opened and in they came, back from a day of hunting.

"Mother, they're here," George announced as soon as they had stepped inside the house.

The family gathered around the kitchen table as Mother opened the letter with shaking hands. George peered over her shoulder, looking at the precious mail. The lines of writing were interspersed with thick black lines of ink where the censored words were obscured from view. The censorship was done by military workers. They made sure secretive information wasn't being passed along in the mail.

Dear Father and Mother, the letter began,

I am doing as well as can be expected. I am in good company. I hope you are all safe and healthy at home. I suppose it's harvest time, and I'll be missing my favorite fall weather there. I never made it where I wanted to go, and I don't believe I will get there. The hills where I am are very tall. It's getting colder, but there isn't any snow yet. I'm sure it will arrive soon, though I hear winter here is much warmer than what I am used to at home. Please don't worry, but I wanted to let you know my leg did sustain a small wound in battle. Mother, I promise you it's nothing to worry about. They sent me to the hospital as a precaution. So, now, I have some time to sit down and write this letter. You may get quite a few over the next week or so, as I have nothing else to do.

Mother's voice broke, faltering over the words.

The letter continued below a large, blacked-out paragraph. *I'm sure I'll be out of here soon, good as new. Tell the family I send my greetings. I miss you all and wish you all well.*

Love, Albert.

The family sat in silence for a few moments, imagining Albert tucked away in a foreign hospital, healing from war injuries. Father hugged Mother, wiping the tears from her face.

"Ah, Aina," he said softly, "have no fear. You raised a strong young man in Albert. I am sure he is just fine."

But George could hear the wavering in Father's voice as well.

♦ ♦ ♦

As George lay awake in bed that night, he couldn't help but doubt Father's reassurances. He wished he could travel overseas to visit Albert and make sure he was going to be okay.

He thought back to the contents of the letter, which he had read over and over again all evening until he had it memorized. *"The hills where I am are very tall. It's getting colder, but there isn't any snow yet. I'm sure it will arrive soon, though I hear winter here is much warmer than what I am used to at home."*

George and Taavi figured Albert was trying to tell them that he would never make it to Finland to talk to White Death as he had hoped, and that he was currently in Italy. He was probably south of Rome, fighting with the Allies as they continued their offensive north toward the ancient city to liberate it from Hitler's control. After Mother had read the letter, they went to the barn to erase the stick figure of Albert in Africa so they could move it to the tip of Italy's boot.

Now, George tossed and turned under the quilt. He rolled over, trying to find a comfortable position on the bed he shared with Robert. Giving up on sleep, he listened to the voices rising up the stairs. Father's soft voice, barely audible. Mother's firm but gentle words. And Taavi's slightly louder but still quiet tone.

"I have to, Mother. I can't in good conscience stay here when Albert and the other boys are out there getting wounded. If I get another draft request, I'm going to go," said Taavi.

"But the mines. You are helping in the mines. The war needs you there. The copper is vital to winning," she protested.

"There are plenty of other men who will take my place in the mines. Those too young, or too old, or unable to pass the physical test to join."

Father's voice was too soft for George to discern his words, but Mother agreed with whatever he said.

"I understand," said Taavi, "but it doesn't feel right. My little brother is injured somewhere over in Europe, and I feel like I can't do anything to help him. At least this way, we are both doing our part."

The conversation continued for a while longer. George's stomach churned. He didn't want another brother to go away to war. He knew he wasn't going to fall asleep anytime soon. With Albert injured and Taavi possibly heading off to fight, his head ached with worry.

13

Poop Flies and Pumpkin Pies
October 1943

George whistled a tune as he walked home from *The Suomi Times* printshop on Saturday morning. He had collected his monthly earnings from his boss, Gurney Mills, and the coins jingled in his pocket. Two dollars would go to Mother, and George would keep fifteen cents. It was a long wait from payday to payday, especially when the soda fountain at Ruska's restaurant called to him so loudly. He usually spent his money in a matter of days, and the wait to get paid again was, at times, agonizing.

Today, though, he couldn't stop at Ruska's for his usual orange soda and pastry. Mother needed him at home to help bring in the last of the squash from the garden.

As he neared the end of Fifth Street, he glanced to his right. A pit of cold dread filled his stomach. There, silent as a winter's night, the Western Union man raised his hand to knock on a door.

The Western Union man only brought bad news. George's heart ached for the people inside, soon to be notified that the worst had happened to a soldier they loved overseas. He ducked his head as the front door of the house opened. He didn't look. But he couldn't block his ears to tune out the cry of grief that pierced the air.

He hurried home, no longer whistling, crossing his fingers that Albert was safe.

As he neared home, he heard the unmistakable rattle and rumble of the honey wagon making its way down Pine Street.

"The honey dippers are almost here, Mother," he said as he went inside and put his two dollars on the kitchen table. "They're on Pine Street, probably two more stops before they get to our house."

"I think I've timed these pies perfectly," said Mother. "They should be just about done by the time Lefty and Cruz finish."

George's stomach grumbled as he looked at the pumpkin pies his mother had spent the morning preparing. They were ready to go into the oven, and by the time the honey dippers finished their job emptying the outhouse, the fresh aroma of baked pumpkin would be filling the air. Mother always made pumpkin pies on the day the honey dippers came. She said the pumpkins and spices kept the stench out of the house.

"Eva, are you going to come outside and watch the honey dippers?" George asked his sister, who was busy knitting in the recliner.

"Absolutely not!" she said.

His sisters were utterly disgusted by the prospect of watching the outhouse get pumped clean, but George thought it was a fascinating job. Usually, Taavi or Albert helped the honey dippers. But now that Albert was away at war and Taavi was working in the copper mine, the task was left to George and Robert. He knew his sisters wouldn't want to help, but he couldn't resist teasing.

"Mary? Catherine?" George grinned, already knowing what their answers would be.

They scrunched their noses and shook their heads.

"I'll stay inside with the pies," said Catherine.

"Me, too," agreed Mary. "I have no interest in the outdoor smells today."

George and Robert ran outside as the honey dippers rattled into the yard.

"Hiya, lads," Cruz greeted them in his loud, boisterous voice.

"Hi, Cruz. Hi, Lefty," George waved as the tractor rumbled across the yard toward the outhouse.

Cruz hopped down from the tractor, his gray beard blowing in the chilly breeze. Wrinkles lined his old face. For as long as George could remember, Cruz had come by every fall to empty their outhouse. Every year, Cruz had a helper, and for the past few years, that helper had been Lefty.

"Hi, boys," Lefty said as he hopped down from his perch on the wagon tongue.

He waved his stump arm, and the boys laughed.

"Where'd you leave your hand today, Lefty?" asked Robert.

"Golly." Lefty feigned shock as he looked at his arm that was missing below his elbow. "Cruz, I did it again. I think we'll need to go back to Mr. Larson's privy and fish it out of the tank."

The boys laughed again. Lefty was always joking about his missing hand. He had lost it in a terrible mining accident a few years back. George's brother, Taavi, remembered that somber day. Accidents were a frequent occurrence in the mines. Some were worse than others. The one that had claimed Lefty's hand had also taken the life of another miner, so Lefty was always talking about his good fortune of just losing one hand.

"All right, boys," said Cruz, "let's see what we're working with today."

He propped open the door of the outhouse. Flies buzzed about, and the pungent odor washed over George and Robert, but Cruz didn't even flinch as he walked inside.

"Looks good and full. Your mother called for us just in time," Cruz announced. "Lefty, grab the hose and start the pump."

The boys watched as one-handed Lefty worked as fast and efficiently as any two-handed person. He curled the hose in the crook of his elbow and unrolled it across the ground. One end of the hose was attached to a large holding tank secured on the flatbed trailer. He gave the free end of the hose to Cruz, who fed it down into the outhouse pit.

"Fire it up!" Cruz hollered to Lefty.

Lefty put a foot on the motor. He used his one good hand to grab the pull cord. He yanked hard, causing the pump's engine to roar to life.

The noise was deafening. George and Robert covered their ears with their palms as Cruz and Lefty pushed the hose deeper into the outhouse pit. The hose sucked up the waste in big slurping gulps, depositing it into the holding tank behind the tractor.

George swatted overhead as swarms of flies escaped their previously comfortable home, now flustered as their warm and cozy residence disappeared up the hose.

After several minutes of slurping, Cruz hollered to Lefty to shut off the motor. The pump sputtered to a stop.

"Grab the lime," Cruz ordered.

Lefty heaved a large burlap sack over his shoulder and grabbed a silver scoop that hung on the side of the tractor. He went into the outhouse and sprinkled a thick layer of powdered lime into the pit to help keep the odors at bay.

"You're all set, boys," Lefty said as he closed the sack.

"Good for another year," added Cruz.

"I'll go tell Mother you're done," said George. He ran into the house so Mother could get money to pay the honey dippers.

"Helena, Cruz said he's hiring," George teased his oldest sister, who was busy making whipped cream for the pumpkin pies. "I know you've been looking for a new job. Why don't you be a honey dipper?"

"I refuse to do such a disgusting job," she said, pushing soft ringlets away from her face.

"Oh, come on. It's not that bad. You'd get to enjoy the beautiful fall weather as you went from outhouse to outhouse, breathing in the wonderful aromas and swatting poop flies from your face all day."

Eva laughed with George as Helena wrinkled her nose.

"I'd rather work in the mines before being a honey dipper," Helena said with disgust.

"But Cruz has been a honey dipper ever since he was a boy. And he told me he's never been sick before. Never. He says the smell scares all the germs away."

"I don't care. Now, go get the money from Mother so that stinky rig can get out of our yard. I don't want to see it anymore, and we don't need any poop flies coming into this house. We all know the flies follow that rig like it's nobody's business."

"What's all this unladylike talk?" Mother asked as she entered the kitchen.

"Helena was just telling me that she wants to be a honey dipper," George said with a smile.

"Did not! Mother, the honey dippers need to get paid. They're waiting outside."

"Maybe I'll be a honey dipper," said George wistfully. "I hate getting sick. I'd rather ride that tractor than be stuck sick in bed."

"Well, being a honey dipper is an honest job. If that's what you wish to do, then, by all means, go for it. But you might be able to find a job that smells a little more pleasant." Mother ruffled his hair. "However, please tell Cruz and Lefty that we are ever so grateful they do the job they do. Make sure they remembered to put down the lime. If they're all done, you can pay them."

She pushed the money into George's hand, and he scooted out the door.

14

Another Draft Card
November 1943

George and Robert were tossing the football back and forth in the yard when Taavi came home from work. It wasn't yet suppertime—unusually early for him to be home. His head was down, and he didn't even notice the boys until George said hello.

"G'afternoon," Taavi said, ducking his head as he took the back steps in one leap and hurried inside.

"That's strange," said George. "I wonder what's happened?"

"You don't suppose another mine accident?" asked Robert.

"Could be. Come on, let's find out."

The boys left the ball in the grass and hurried inside after Taavi.

They quietly pushed the door open and heard Mother crying. The boys stopped in the entryway, silently shutting the door behind them as they listened to the conversation in the kitchen.

"I can't defer my enlistment any longer, Mother," Taavi was telling her.

"Yes, yes, you have to. Please don't go. Please," she was sobbing.

George's stomach turned to knots.

"This is my third draft request. I was fine deferring the other two, but they obviously need me. This war needs me. Men are getting injured and dying every day. You read Albert's letter. They need replacements. I have to go. I *want* to go."

Mother's quiet cries filled the silence.

Father spoke. "It's okay, Aina. The Good Lord will watch over our boys. If Taavi feels this is best, we have to let him go."

"Ah, but it's so hard to let them go. You may be my eldest, but you're still my little boy."

By Taavi's muffled reply, George knew Mother was hugging him tightly.

With a lump in his throat, he grabbed Robert by the arm and pulled him back outside before anyone knew they had been eavesdropping. His head was spinning, and neither of the boys were in the mood to play catch anymore. So, they sat on the cold ground next to the garden and watched in heavy silence as two squirrels scurried through the fallen leaves in search of some last-minute acorns to stash away for winter.

♦ ♦ ♦

In the week leading up to Taavi's departure, George and his family spent as much time with him as possible. He had quit his job in the copper mine, so he was home all day. Their mother even let the children skip school on Thursday and Friday to be with him before his train departed on Saturday.

On Friday afternoon, Taavi called George to the barn.

"I guess this is all yours now," he motioned to the map on the worktable. "I trust you'll keep up on our progress."

George nodded, but he held back tears at the thought of keeping the map updated without Taavi.

"You'll be safe?" George whispered to his oldest brother.

"Safer than that dollar tucked away in your drawer from the potato harvest," he teased.

George tried to smile at the joke, but he was too worried.

"Now, remember, I'm going to be on the opposite side of the world from Albert. So don't forget about me." He pointed to the Pacific Ocean. "It might be harder to track my movement since the navy ships aren't contained to land like the battles in Europe, but I'll do my best to give you hints in my letters."

He pointed to the map and drew an imaginary circle in the bottom left corner. "From the sounds of things, most of the action has been in the South Pacific, but no guarantees it'll stay that way."

"Where do you ship out of?" George asked, dread settling onto his chest like a heavy anchor.

"After my training is finished in Chicago, I'll head to San Francisco. I'll ship out from there. But don't worry, it'll be a long ship ride west before we see any action."

Taavi rolled up the map and put it back in the cardboard tube. "Just promise me you'll keep this hidden from Mother."

"You promise me you'll stay safe," George countered.

"Deal." Taavi smiled and held out his hand.

George stuck out his hand to shake Taavi's, but instead, his older brother pulled him in for an embrace.

"Be strong, Yrjö. Mother needs you now more than ever before. And remember to help Father with the chores. He doesn't need to be doing everything by himself."

"I will."

♦ ♦ ♦

George and Robert played one last evening of checkers with Taavi before Saturday's noon train came to take him away.

"King me!" Robert said as he pushed his piece to the other side of the board.

"Good job," said Taavi. "You boys are really getting the hang of this game. I suspect, by the time I return, you'll be able to whoop me good."

"Do you think you'll be able to play checkers on the navy ships?" George asked.

"I reckon so, if there's a board. Although, maybe we'll be too busy fighting the Japanese to play much."

"But you'll write to us, letting us know how things are going and where you are?" asked Robert.

"Well, the mail censorship won't let any specific location information through, but I'll do my best to let you know where I am and how things are going."

The game continued in relative silence for a few minutes. The radio was set at a low volume, alternating between a Western program and war news from the European front.

"You boys better take good care of Mother," Taavi said in a

low voice. "I know she worries plenty with Albert gone. And once I leave, I have a feeling it'll be extra hard on her. Be good boys. Don't be causing any unnecessary trouble for her."

"We'll be good," promised George.

Robert nodded in agreement.

The boys played checkers late into the night. Neither Mother nor Father chided them about being up past their bedtime. Finally, when Robert fell asleep at the table in the middle of a move, Taavi instructed them to head up to bed.

Feet heavy and stomach churning, George climbed the steps and huddled under the blankets with Robert. Taavi lingered a while longer downstairs with their parents. George waited to fall asleep until Taavi came upstairs and settled into the bed on the other side of the room.

♦ ♦ ♦

The noon train barreled into the station promptly on time. George was sorely disappointed. He had spent the restless night hoping it would have jumped the tracks somewhere south of town. To no avail, it chugged into town with brakes squealing and black clouds billowing.

Mother had cried all morning at home but managed to dry her tears for the walk through town to the train station. She started crying again as they climbed the steps to the platform. Once she started, it was a chain reaction with the sisters. George's stomach was in knots as he readied to say goodbye to another brother.

"Oh, Taavi. We will miss you. Be safe, my sweet boy." Mother fussed at his clothes and hair.

"I'll be just fine, Mother. You don't need to waste your worries on me."

One by one, the siblings took turns hugging Taavi and saying their goodbyes. The lump in George's throat grew bigger with each passing moment, until it was his turn.

"Bye, Yrjö." Taavi hugged him. "I'll miss you. Keep up with your schoolwork. Be sure to help Father and Mother with the chores. Keep your chin up and be strong."

George nodded, but the tears started to leak from his eyes. He couldn't hold them back anymore. He didn't want Taavi to leave. He wanted his entire family back home, safe and warm, where no one was halfway around the world fighting in the war.

"It's okay," reassured Taavi. "I promise I'll be back before you know it. And by the time I get home, I'm sure you'll whoop me a good one at checkers. I'll see you soon." He tousled George's hair and used his sleeve to wipe the tears from George's cheeks.

The family stood back, watching Taavi enter the train the same way Albert had earlier that summer. He held his head high and gave one last salute. Then, he boarded the train and headed off to join the war.

◆ ◆ ◆

That night, George and Robert played the most silent game of checkers their house had ever witnessed. The radio played George's favorite Western program, but he paid no attention to it. And even though he beat Robert five games to four, there was no happiness left in him to gloat.

"You boys best get on up to bed," Mother said as the clock chimed nine times.

"Yes, Mother," they mumbled.

The benches on either side of the pine table scraped across the wood floor. The boys performed their nightly routine of washing their hands and faces, brushing their teeth, saying prayers with Mother and Father, climbing the stairs, and getting into their pajamas. The girls joined in the routine, though they turned right at the top of the stairs instead of left.

"I guess I'll take Taavi's bed," George said as he and Robert looked into their quiet bedroom.

Not too long ago, George remembered dreaming of a time when he wouldn't have to share a bed anymore. But now that Albert and Taavi were gone, and he and Robert would each have a bed to themselves, it just didn't feel right. He'd gladly sleep four to a bed tonight, if only it meant he'd have his brothers home.

George slipped under the covers into Taavi's bed. They smelled faintly of the mines, the same scent that lingered on Taavi's clothes after a workday. He was glad laundry day was a full week away. He crossed his fingers that Mother would forget to wash the sheets on this bed.

He reached through the darkness for his clothes folded on the floor next to the bed. From his pocket, he pulled out the pencil that he had taken from Taavi's workbench. He closed his eyes and squeezed his fingers tightly around it. He hadn't had the heart to draw a stick figure symbolizing Taavi in Chicago yet. Maybe tomorrow.

It took a while, but eventually sleep allowed his worried mind to drift into unconsciousness.

15

Ungrateful Thanksgiving
November 1943

"That's not fair!" Eva said as George tagged her arm and kept running across the slippery ice of the frozen dam.

Eva tried to change directions to chase after him, arms spinning like pinwheels, but she tripped and fell onto the slick ice.

"Ouch," she moaned.

"Come on, hurry!" said Mary through her giggles. "Mother will be here any minute to tell us to come home."

"I'm trying," Eva said, "but these boots have no grip. I can barely get started, and once I do, I can't stop." She stomped her foot in frustration.

Mary held out a hand to help her sister. "Here, take my spot." Then Mary dashed across the smooth ice in pursuit of George.

The frozen dam was filled with children from town playing a game of ships and islands in the morning sunshine. It was a beautiful morning for the Thanksgiving holiday. Mother had shooed the younger children outside to get fresh air and burn off some energy before their big dinner with the family.

"Can I join?" a loud voice boomed from the trees along the frozen shoreline.

"Uncle Roy!" George shouted with excitement.

He ran as fast as his legs could carry him over the slippery ice. Eva, Catherine, Mary, and Robert followed close behind.

"How are my favorite nieces and nephews?" he asked as the children barreled into him.

Over the excited din of welcoming and questions, Uncle Roy laughed and told the children it was time to come home for Thanksgiving dinner.

"Your mother and older sisters have prepared quite the feast. Best hurry home so we can eat while it's still hot. There'll be plenty of time to talk after dinner."

As they went inside and removed their heavy outerwear, George looked longingly at the bare counter. In years past, it had been filled with pies. But the war had caused a shortage of flour this month, so that meant no Thanksgiving pies.

Instead, he gazed at the kitchen table, which was filled with turkey, ham, potatoes, beans, corn, stuffing, gravy, and apple slices. There was more than enough food, and he knew he couldn't complain. He was grateful for such a feast. But that didn't stop the little twinge of disappointment from lingering in his chest as he longed for pie.

"Hard to keep from snitching a little bite, isn't it, George?" Aunt Doris put her arm around his shoulders and pulled him close. "Good to see you again. You've certainly grown since we last visited. Your mother will have to start putting bricks on your head to keep you from growing through the roof."

George laughed. "Good to see you, too, Aunt Doris. How was your trip?"

"Oh, it was long, as usual. But we only had two flat tires and no engine problems, so I'll call it a success."

Aunt Doris and Uncle Roy had driven all the way from Detroit to visit George's family. It took an entire day to drive the distance. Since rations for gasoline and tires were scarce, they hadn't visited in over a year.

"All right, now," Mother said, clasping her hands together, "let us sit and eat before it all goes cold. Solomon, grace, please?"

Everyone bowed their heads as George's father said a short prayer. He offered thanks for their good fortune with the harvest this year and asked the Good Lord to watch over the soldiers fighting overseas."

"Amen," said George as he filled his plate with the Thanksgiving feast.

For a few minutes, the only sounds in the kitchen were the crackle of the fire and the clink of dinnerware as they ate the delicious Thanksgiving dinner. Finally, Uncle Roy spoke.

"How are you faring now that your older boys aren't home?"

"There's a bit more for me to do around the house, but nothing that can't be managed," Father said.

"The food lasts longer," Mother laughed. "I think those two boys ate as much as the rest of us combined."

"And the work?" Uncle Roy asked.

"They send home their earnings, so it helps. War doesn't pay as well as the copper mines, but we're making do," said Father.

"You know, there are some great opportunities in Detroit. The war factories are in desperate need of hands. They pay top dollar, too. I'd be more than happy to lend a bedroom."

"I appreciate the offer, Roy," said Father, "but the bakery is doing well right now. Besides, I can't leave Aina, and the children are in school."

"Oh, I wasn't meaning you. Forgive me, but I was speaking of your older girls."

Helena, Elaine, and Ann all looked up from their meals, forks paused in midair.

"They hire girls in the factories now?" Helena asked, her bright blue eyes sparkling.

"Of course," said Roy. "All the boys have been called to fight. No one's left in town but the women to run the factories and build the war equipment. Tanks, airplanes, missiles, guns—you name it, the women are building it."

"Oh, Mother, may we please go?" Helena begged. "You know I've always wanted to go to a big city. Please?"

Mother shook her head. "I'm sorry, but I need you here," she said. "Besides, you have a perfectly good job that pays very well."

"I don't like my job at all. You know that. I hate cleaning Mr. Bogg's house, and his children are nearly feral."

"Watch your words, Helena," Father warned, as she scowled and crossed her arms over her chest.

"Please, Mother?" Elaine joined in. "We could make so much more money there. We'd send it all back. Every penny."

"We could buy you a washing machine!" Ann added, her braids bobbing against her shoulders as she squirmed with excitement in her seat.

Mother smiled at the thought. "I'm glad you're all so eager to help, but just the thought of sending three of my girls away while two of my boys are already gone makes my heart hurt."

"Oh, come on—" started Helena.

"That's enough, girls," said Father, as he held his hands up. "Roy, thank you for the offer, but right now it's just not possible. Aina needs the girls here, and a strange city is no place for three young ladies to be living."

That silenced the chatter for the remainder of the Thanksgiving meal.

As they cleared the table, Ann whispered to George, "It's not fair. The boys get to go off and help win the war, but we aren't allowed to just because we're girls. I want to go to Detroit. I want to work in a war factory. I'd make a lot of money and send it all back so you could buy whatever you wanted."

George thought for a moment. "If I could buy anything in the world, it would be a pair of ice skates."

"Exactly," said Ann. "You could buy anything you wanted if we were able to work in a factory and send the money back home."

"That's enough complaining for one Thanksgiving, Ann," Mother scolded. "We may not have much in this house, but we always have enough."

Ann turned red in the face, unaware that Mother had been listening to her complaints.

"Sorry, ma'am," she mumbled. "I just thought it would have been fun to go on an adventure."

"I understand," said Mother, "but we must not forget to be grateful for the things we already have."

George agreed that they must be grateful for what they had, but it didn't hurt to wish for a pair of ice skates.

♦ ♦ ♦

That evening, after second helpings had been eaten and every belly was filled with the wonderful Thanksgiving food, George walked to the Pine Street ice rink with his siblings. The rink was an outdoor sheet of ice that the local children constructed as soon as the weather turned cold enough. It was situated in a clearing between the railroad tracks and the north side of Pine Street. The snow had been packed down tightly and then flooded with water to create a thick sheet of ice.

George and his siblings slid across the smooth surface on their boots and raced in circles with the other town children as the streetlights and stars twinkled overhead. As evening grew into night, the hockey games began. The children wearing boots had to get off the ice to make way for the teams to play hockey. Every evening, as long as the winter was cold enough to keep the ice frozen, teams would play hockey games well into the night. George watched intently from the third row of the bleachers, taking in every motion and movement of the skaters.

"It must be like flying," he said dreamily to Ann.

"Don't worry, Yrjö," she whispered back to him. "I'll get you a pair of ice skates, even if I have to walk to Detroit myself."

16

Detroit or Bust
December 1943

George slid through the quiet forest on his wooden cross-country skis. He enjoyed the muted stillness of the winter woodlands, especially after a fresh snowfall. Fluffy flakes were mounded in piles on the pine branches, causing them to sag under the weight. Chickadees swooped low through the snow-covered forest, searching for any small morsel of food to fill their hungry bellies. A cardinal perched high in a tree, its brilliant red feathers shining like a beacon against the white backdrop.

It was Saturday, and also Uncle Roy and Aunt Doris's last night in town. The sulking from his three oldest sisters was at an all-time high, so George had escaped the gloomy mood in the house and slipped into the forest for some peace and quiet. His sisters were adamant that they wanted to move to Detroit to work in the factories producing war supplies. And Mother was just as adamant to keep them safely at home, away from the large, bustling, and sometimes dangerous city.

George stayed in the woods as long as he could. All too soon, the biting cold began to sting his cheeks, so he turned his skis toward home. The smoke rising from the chimney was an inviting sight as he turned off the ski path and headed down the street.

"He's here, Mother." Eva peeked her head into the back room as George unbundled his winter gear. "Hurry up," she beckoned to George. "We got another letter from Finland. Mother was waiting until you got back to read it."

"Be right there," he said, leaving his winter gear in a haphazard mess on the floor in his rush to get to the living room.

The family gathered around Mother's chair near the hearth as she opened the letter. The crackling fire brought some much-needed warmth to George's chilled hands and face.

My dearest Aina,

Words cannot express my gratitude for your delightful package that arrived in the post. It was an absolute joy to open! The baby clothes are keeping the little one warm during our cold and snowy winter. And oh, the money. Ten whole dollars! It was enough to buy us meat to last much of the winter, providing the Good Lord doesn't make this one drag out too long. And come spring, we will plant those wonderful little seeds in our garden and look forward to the bounty in the fall.

The mail censorship had blacked out all but the last few lines of the next paragraph. *We wish you and the children well. We miss you every day but know you're in better hands in America. Give the children kisses.*

Love,

Äiti.

Mother's soft voice faded as the letter ended, her eyes staring unfocused out the window.

"You miss them, don't you, Mother?" Robert asked.

"Yes, yes, I do."

"Will you tell us about the ship ride over, please?" Helena asked. "You haven't told that story in so long."

"Ah, no. Not today. Besides, you children know that story better than I do by now," Mother said as she wiped tears from her eyes.

"But you tell it best," said Elaine.

A chorus of voices joined in, begging Mother to tell the story of when she came to America.

"All right, children. If you insist, I will tell it again."

George sat on the wood floor at Mother's feet. He never tired of hearing her stories.

"It was nearing harvest time," Mother began. "We had another horrible crop failure. It was the third year in a row. There was no rain. The stream behind our house was bone dry."

"And all the crops were lost?" Robert asked.

"Nearly every single one. We salvaged a few of the root vegetables since they weren't as prone to the scorching sun. But we could barely even call it a harvest."

"So, then what?" asked Eva.

"Then, I sat down with my father and mother and asked them what we were going to do. There were too many mouths to feed. We had just a small amount of money left. So, I offered to leave. I would go to America. My uncle was already here. He owned a sawmill in Minnesota. He often wrote to us, telling us there was work available. My two older brothers had gone a few years back, before the drought and crop failures started."

"And they let you go?" asked Mary.

The children all watched Mother intently as they listened to the tale.

"They didn't have much of a choice," said Mother. "It was either that or face starvation over the winter. If I left, there would be one less mouth to feed, and what small amount of food they had could go a little further."

"How did you buy a ticket?"

"Well, we took some money from the small savings my parents had, and I set out for England. It was a long journey. I took what I could by train and small passenger boat, but I also had to walk for many miles. Eventually, I ended up in Liverpool, where I purchased a one-way ticket aboard a ship bound for America by way of Canada."

"And were you sad to leave?" Ann asked.

"Ah, my sweet daughter, you have no idea. I cried and I cried and I cried. I think the ocean levels rose several inches from the tears I cried on that voyage. Many of us on the ship shed tears. We knew we were never going back. We would never see most of the people we left, ever again."

George felt a pang in his chest as he imagined what it would be like to say goodbye to Mother and Father forever.

"What was the ship like?" asked Eva, eyes bright as she listened intently to every word.

"The ship was bigger than anything I'd ever seen. There were three stories of cabins. A red smokestack stood tall, rising up from the middle of the ship. I was below deck in the steerage class, as that's where the cheapest cabins were located. It was very loud from the engines and machinery. And smelly. Many people were seasick, and there weren't enough amenities to clean properly. It was a long week on the open water, and I was so grateful to finally see land again."

"And then what happened?" asked Catherine.

"Then I got on a train and headed west. Far, far west to my uncle's sawmill in the northern forests of Minnesota. There, I worked as a hired hand in the boarding house. I kept his workers fed, the house clean, and the laundry fresh."

The children sat in silence for a moment.

"And how old were you, Mother?" asked Helena.

"I was barely a day over twenty. Hardly old enough to make such a journey on my own, but I was just doing what had to be done."

"So, you were the same age that Elaine is now," Helena said. "And I'm twenty-two. And I know Ann is a bit young, at eighteen, but Mother, you know the feeling. You know what it's like to want to adventure and see the world and do better for your family."

"Yes, my dear. I know." Mother's voice softened to a near whisper.

Helena didn't ask any more questions. But in the silence that followed, Mother knew what she was trying to ask. She paused for a long moment. All the children held their breath. Father and Uncle Roy and Aunt Doris looked at Mother. Father gave her a small nod of his head as if he agreed with her no matter what decision she made.

Finally, Mother spoke.

"Oh, my dear girls. I am going to miss you so much. But if you so desire, and if Roy and Doris promise to take good care of you, I will let you go with them to Detroit."

The room exploded with whoops and cheers and jumping about. Helena hugged Ann. Ann hugged Elaine. Elaine hugged them both. Mother was crying but laughed through her tears. A soft smile tugged at the corners of Father's mouth. The rest of the sisters chatted excitedly about the big adventure about to take place, and Robert ran circles around the chaos.

George smiled as he turned around in front of the fire to warm his feet better. He would miss his sisters, but he was happy they were able to go to Detroit.

Finally, Mother got a grip over the pandemonium.

"Girls, girls," she said. "It's getting late. And oh, my, you leave in the morning. Go pack. You'll need everything. Roy, are you sure you have room in your house for them? And what about enough space in the automobile? They'll need winter clothes and bedding and towels and—"

"Don't worry, Aina." Uncle Roy held up his hands reassuringly and cut her off. "We can fit all their luggage in the trunk, and we can always purchase a few items as needed once we are back in Detroit. We have more than enough room in the house. Both of the upstairs bedrooms are vacant now that our children moved out. It will be nice to have a little action in the house again."

◆ ◆ ◆

In the morning, Mother bustled about, organizing suitcases and outerwear in the trunk of Uncle Roy's automobile. She hugged and kissed each girl time and time again.

"Promise you'll write. Let us know how things are," she begged.

"Of course, we will," Helena reassured her.

"Remember, Aina, we have a telephone," Aunt Doris told her. "Any time you wish to talk, give us a ring. Just walk down to Aunt Elvie's house and phone us."

"Of course, of course," Mother said, her restless hands tugging at the bottom of her apron.

"Have fun, girls." Mother gave them one last hug as they hopped into the back seat of Uncle Roy's automobile. "Be safe."

"We will," they called back in unison.

"You'll have your washing machine in no time," Ann said through the open window.

"And after that, we'll save up for some indoor plumbing," said Elaine with a smile. "I know you'd like that, Mother."

"I think everyone is looking forward to that day," Mother laughed.

George and his remaining family members waved as the automobile roared to life, bumped down their street, and drove away from town.

As they walked to church, he felt an emptiness that he'd never known before. Half of his family was gone. Just a short five months ago, no one had ever left home. Now, it was just George,

Robert, Eva, Mary, and Catherine.

They filed into the church and sat in their usual pew. The end of the bench was vacant, the usual occupants now off to start their new lives. George was happy for his sisters to be going on their adventure, but he was sad that his family was growing up and changing.

If it wasn't for the war, things would have continued as normal. George was torn over his feelings toward the war. He didn't like what it was doing to his family, even if he did want to support his country.

17

Pine Street Ice Rink
December 1943

A knock at the door alerted George to either a visitor or an evening delivery. He opened the back door to find Will's arms laden with a crate of eggs.

"Here's your delivery, sir," said a beaming Will.

"Thank you, Mr. Egg-man, sir," George said with a nod.

The boys exchanged their usual script. Will pretended to be an important elderly deliveryman, and George played along.

"I apologize for the downsize in product, but my hens seem to have gone on strike in this cold weather."

"Can't say I blame them," said George.

"Tell the missus she owes me half the usual cost. I'll add it to her tab. Good day, my lad," Will finished with a dramatic bow.

"Will," said Mother, coming up behind the boys. "Thank you ever so much. And don't worry about half the eggs. Did George tell you we now have half the children in the house? One crate will do just fine for the time being. I don't expect the other children to return home until at least springtime. Tell your hens to stay warm in this frigid weather."

As Will turned to continue on his delivery route, George called out to him, "What time are you done?"

"Probably forty-five minutes. Thirty if I hurry, and if the snowplow finally made it over to the west side of town."

"Do you want to come to the ice rink after? A few of us are going to be playing a game of boot hockey. We have extra hockey sticks."

"Sure, I'll be there."

George watched as Will hurried to Mr. Tinney's delivery truck. Mr. Tinney had been gone to war for almost two months now. Will had taken over his egg delivery route, which included driving the rusty flatbed. Will's short legs had to stretch to their maximum capacity to reach the clutch and pedals, but he managed to steer the truck with precision through the streets once a week on his delivery route. He was the absolute envy of every young boy in town.

♦ ♦ ♦

George quickly finished his evening chores. He had to fill the woodbox with enough logs to last through the night and into the morning. He brought a stack of magazines to the outhouse. Bathroom tissue was expensive, so the magazines that arrived in the mail were a cheaper alternative and did the job just as well, providing the pages were crumpled and softened before use. Finally, he swept the back entryway and mopped up the puddles of water that had formed from melted snow.

He looked at the clock. He needed to leave soon to get to the ice rink, but he switched on the radio to get an update on the Red

Wings hockey game. They were playing today, and he hoped they could pull out a win.

He missed hearing about Sid Abel, who had helped the Red Wings win the Stanley Cup last season. Sid was his favorite player but had left at the end of last season to fight for his country. Even George's beloved hockey team wasn't immune to the effects of war.

"Mother, I'm heading to the ice rink," he told her as he bundled up.

"Be back before bedtime," she replied just before he slammed the door.

George walked the three blocks to the Pine Street ice rink. The lights were already aglow. Children of all ages raced across the ice, sliding and gliding and shooting pucks. He walked around the edge of the rink to the warming house to meet his team.

"Hi, George," they called out to him. Most of his teammates had already gathered.

"Ready to win tonight?" he asked John, who was also on his team.

"We better. It's been a long time since the Green Jackets have lost a game. They're getting a bit too big for their britches around school."

The boys cleared the smaller children off the ice so they could play their game of boot hockey. Boot hockey wasn't as fast or intense as the games played on ice skates. But since many of the children couldn't afford skates, they instead played on their slippery boots.

The game was a tough one, and even though they put up a good fight, George's team wasn't able to win.

"Oh, shucks," said John as they trudged back to the bleachers after the game. "Better luck next time."

"Hey!" Will called from the bleachers, his egg deliveries now complete. "Great job! You almost had them."

"Almost," said George. "We'll beat them sooner or later."

As the night grew colder, the games continued. The three boys sat in the bleachers with other children from town, watching intently. George watched as the players flew around the ice on their hockey skates. They were so incredibly fast, sometimes just blurs whipping by. He wondered what it would feel like to glide on skates.

Between games, or whenever their extremities started to go numb, they would go into the warming house to thaw their hands and toes before going back outside to watch again.

As the teams on the ice changed once again, George noticed a familiar face skating. It was Ricky McClain. George hadn't forgotten Ricky's hurtful words at the start of the school year, especially not the words about Albert having to fight on the front lines just because he was a poor soldier.

Jealousy burned like a lump of red-hot coals in George's chest. It wasn't fair that someone like Ricky, who was so mean and cruel, could afford skates and play real hockey. Ricky didn't know what it was like to be stuck on boots, just slipping and sliding, instead of gliding with ease.

As if hearing his thoughts, Ricky skated past the bleachers, gloating as he went. He made a loop around the rink for his warm-up lap, this time skating as fast as he could when he neared the boys. Ricky came right toward them, then turned his feet and dug his blades into the ice. He came to a quick stop, spraying a cloud of icy snow into their faces.

"Hey, now," yelled John.

"Watch it!" added Will.

George's face heated up in anger as he wiped off the snow spray.

"Why don't you boys get on the ice and give it a whirl?" Ricky taunted. "Oh, yeah, I forgot. You need *these*." He pointed to his skates.

"Go away, Ricky," said John. "You smell, your pants are too tight, and you're not even good at hockey."

Ricky pretended not to hear. "Maybe if your parents weren't so poor, you'd be able to afford skates so you could play hockey."

George held his tongue. He knew Mother would be very upset if he started a fight. But the frustration bubbling inside him was too much.

He reached down to the snowbank in front of him and packed a solid ball between his mittened hands. Just as Ricky turned to skate away, George let the snowball fly. It landed smack dab on Ricky's head, knocked him off balance, and caused him to fall onto the ice with a thud.

"Joke's on you, Ricky," Will shouted after him. "I don't have any parents."

The boys scurried away before Ricky could cause an even

bigger scene.

"Come on," said Will. "Want to learn how to drive Tinney's truck?"

George and John agreed that learning how to drive Mr. Tinney's truck would be infinitely more fun than watching Ricky play hockey. Will drove them to the dirt road on the other side of the dam so they could practice driving without being near the vehicles and buildings of town. George and John took turns behind the wheel, learning how to let out the clutch just enough so the truck shifted smoothly from gear to gear.

George knew that, although Ricky was mean, he was right. His parents were too poor to buy frivolous items such as hockey skates. But he would bet the crisp dollar tucked away in his drawer from the potato harvest that Ricky didn't have a single true friend. And especially not a friend who could teach him how to drive a truck.

"Do you think Mr. Tinney would mind if I drove this back to the ice rink?" George asked as he gripped the wheel, released the clutch, and pressed down on the gas.

"Go ahead. You're already as smooth as a whistle on the gears," said Will.

George steered the truck through the few streets back into town. The previous hockey game had just ended, and the players were standing between the warming house and the road. He saw Ricky and chuckled at the thought of the snowball knocking him to the ice.

He slowed as he drove the truck past the crowd of boys and

rolled down the window.

"Hey, Ricky," George called through the open window.

Ricky and the rest of the boys turned to look.

"Maybe if your parents weren't so poor, you'd be able to afford a truck so you could drive."

Ricky opened his mouth to retort, but George let out the clutch and roared away in the truck, covering the crowd of boys in black exhaust fumes.

The three boys in the truck doubled over with laughter. George was laughing so hard he nearly steered off the street and into a snowbank.

"Oh, you should've seen his face," John howled with laughter. "I've never seen such a shocked look on someone."

The boys laughed all the way to the other end of town, where George pulled to the side of the road to let Will take over the driving. George and John hopped out and walked back down Pine Street to their homes, leaving Will to drive Mr. Tinney's truck back to the valley.

The entire walk home, George and John chuckled. Though it made him feel a little better by giving Ricky a taste of his own medicine, George still longed to fly on the ice.

He knew Ann would pull through on her promise. Someday, somehow, he would get a pair of ice skates.

18

Merry Christmas
December 1943

"How about this one?" Robert asked, pointing to a scraggly pine tree.

"No, that's too bare. Mother said to get a nice full one," George responded.

"Up ahead, boys," their father said, "we're bound to find a good one in that clearing."

George and Robert trailed after him as he pulled a makeshift sled through the tall drifts.

"This one," George said, standing beside a full spruce tree. "This is the perfect Christmas tree."

"I reckon you're right," said Father as he dropped the rope that pulled the thin sheet of tin. "Want to cut it?"

George nodded, grabbed the saw, and crawled under the snowy boughs. Cold flakes tickled the back of his neck as he knocked snow loose, but he didn't mind. It was almost Christmas! And while half of his siblings weren't going to be home, it was still his favorite time of year.

Soon enough, the tree was cut down, loaded onto the sheet of tin, and they began to trudge back through the snow toward home.

"My goodness!" Mother exclaimed as they brought it through the back door. "What a delightful tree!"

"I picked it out," said George as he brushed a clump of snow from a branch.

"And I helped," said Robert, bouncing on his toes with excitement.

"You both did a wonderful job. Now, let's find the ornaments and get this decorated."

George and Robert ran to the barn in the backyard and climbed into the loft. Tucked away near the rafters were two large cardboard boxes filled with Christmas decorations. They carefully took them down and brought them back into the house.

"Remember this one?" Mother asked George as she opened the first box and held up a snowman made of cotton balls. "This was the very first ornament you gave me. You made it in Mrs. Schultz's kindergarten class."

"I remember," said George, taking the ornament and hanging it front and center on the tree.

"And here's the little reindeer that Taavi carved in woodshop his senior year," Catherine said as she leaned in to help.

"Albert made the same one a few years later," Mary said, pulling out a matching reindeer.

"And these knitted snowflakes that you girls made," Mother said, pulling out a string of six sparkling white snowflakes.

The family reminisced on Christmases past as they pulled every single ornament and decoration out of the boxes and placed them on the tree and around the house.

After they had finished, they crowded into the kitchen to make a fresh batch of ginger cookies. Mr. Jenkins, the grocer, had even been able to spare a small bag of white chocolate, and George helped his mother melt it in a small pot over the woodstove to drizzle on the warm cookies.

"Just one week until Christmas," Father announced over the din of laughter and conversation as he looked at the calendar.

"Do you think the soldiers will get to have a Christmas celebration?" Robert asked.

The lively room went quiet. All the children looked at Father and Mother.

"Yes, I believe they will celebrate Christmas," Mother said, though George saw a cloud of doubt pass over her eyes. "It may not be with the usual touches like they're used to, but I would think the generals would be nice enough to let the soldiers have a little party."

George thought for a moment, then asked his mother, "Can we write Albert and Taavi another letter and ask them how they get to celebrate Christmas?"

"That is a fine idea," agreed Mother.

The children sat down at the kitchen table as the rest of the cookies finished baking. They each took a scrap of paper and wrote a letter or drew a picture for their brothers. Once done, Mother sealed them into two envelopes—one for each brother away fighting in the war.

"Shall we go together to mail them?" she asked.

A chorus of voices agreed, eager to stroll along the streets of town to the post office.

Snow crunched under George's boots as he shoved his hands deeper into the pockets of his jacket. It was cold, but he did his best to ignore it. He was too busy gazing into all the festively decorated shop windows. Garland draped the window frames, small Christmas trees were propped up in a few of the storefronts, and paper snowflakes dangled from the ceilings. Some stores even had puffs of cotton lining the bottoms of their displays to look like snow.

They arrived at the post office, cheeks rosy-red from the cold. The little bell on the door jingled merrily as they bustled into the small room.

"My, oh my," said the jolly postmaster. "What did I do to deserve such fine company on such a cold day?"

"We're here to mail some letters," Eva said as she handed the white envelopes over the counter.

"I see," he replied, reading the addresses. "And very important letters at that."

"Think they'll get there in time for Christmas?" George asked hopefully.

"There is a chance, young man," the postmaster replied. "If Taavi is still training in the States, his should arrive in time. But I'm not so confident about Albert's reaching Europe before Christmas. The quickest they get there is just under a week. But I've seen them take as long as a month. Regardless, I'm sure your brothers will be pleased no matter when they receive them."

George nodded.

"And if you'll all wait here, I have a surprise for you."

He disappeared through the swinging door into the back room, returning a few moments later with a large, brown box.

"Arrived just last night on the truck. I'm sure it's full of wonderful surprises." He winked and pushed the box across the counter.

"What is it? Who is it from?" George asked as he bounced on his tippy toes.

"It's from Detroit," Mother said. "Let's not waste a minute. Time to get this home right away."

Father carried the box all the way home and set it on the kitchen table. Mother grabbed a sharp knife and slid it over the brown tape that held the edges closed.

"Oh, my," she exclaimed. "What a wonderful surprise. It's from Helena, Elaine, and Ann."

One by one, Mother lifted five brown packages from the box and handed them to each of the children.

"Can we open them now, Mother? Please?" Robert begged.

"I think not," Mother teased, a twinkle in her eyes. "Those are for Christmas morning. Go put them under the tree."

George turned his present over and over in his hands, trying to guess what was inside. It was soft. About the size of a small loaf of bread. His name was written in script on the front. It was Elaine's handwriting.

Robert was shaking his and trying to peek under the brown paper flaps that kept the present concealed.

"You heard your mother," Father said gently. "Your gifts can wait under the tree until Christmas morning."

"In the meantime," said Mother, "let's enjoy this delicious caramel popcorn they sent."

She pulled a bag of golden popcorn from the bottom of the box. The children reluctantly placed their parcels under the tree, but handfuls of the sweet, sticky treat were a tasty distraction.

That evening, once the chores were finished, George slipped into the barn to update the war progress on Taavi's map. He took off his mittens and breathed on his fingers. The barn sheltered him from the wind and snow, but not from the cold.

He had done his best to keep up with the progress of the Allies, but every time he came to the barn and unrolled the map, his heart was heavy, and worry filled his mind. They hadn't received a letter from Taavi saying he had shipped out of San Francisco yet, so George crossed his fingers in hopes that he was still safe from the bombs and bullets in the Pacific.

♦ ♦ ♦

In the days that followed, George spent his time going to school, watching hockey at the Pine Street ice rink, hauling in endless amounts of firewood to keep the house warm, and keeping a close eye on the brown package with his name on it that lay under the Christmas tree.

Every morning before leaving for school, he picked it up. Every lunch hour when he ran home to eat and listen to the noon war updates on the radio, he gave it a few shakes. And every evening after he and Robert played checkers, they examined their presents together. Soon enough, small holes started to tear in the paper. George could see his present was made of green material. Robert's was blue. Catherine, Mary, and Eva had also poked small holes in their wrapping paper.

Mother laughed at their impatience, but she still didn't allow them to open their gifts.

On Christmas Eve, the family spent the evening at church attending their Christmas service. George joined his Sunday school class at the front of the church as they sang Christmas hymns in front of the congregation.

Finally, after what felt like the longest week of his life, Christmas Eve night arrived, and it was time for their last sleep before Christmas morning.

"You may hang your stockings, children," Mother said as they were getting ready for bed.

George raced upstairs to find his biggest wool sock. Once everyone had found a suitable stocking, they tacked them to the mantle to await the gifts that would appear overnight.

Long after Father went to bed, and long after Mother went to bed, and long after the moon traced a wide arc across the night sky, sleep finally overtook the excitement and anticipation for morning, and George drifted off.

♦ ♦ ♦

"It's pajamas!" George shouted with glee as he tore the brown wrapping paper off the present that had been waiting under the Christmas tree. Inside, rolled up tightly, was a pair of thick, green flannel pajamas.

"Unroll it," Robert said excitedly. "There's more!"

"A new shirt!" George exclaimed as he unrolled the pajamas and a blue and white plaid shirt fell into his lap. "It still has the tags on," he added as he looked down at the crisp white price tag dangling from the shirt sleeve. The price had been scribbled out, but the tag was fresh and new and from a real store.

He had never owned a new shirt before. It was usually hand-me-downs from his older brothers. And when clothes were scarce and Mother had to buy him something, it was from Cheap Joe's, the secondhand store in town.

"Did you see it still has the tags on?" Robert asked with an awe-filled voice.

"Yes," George whispered as he rubbed his fingers over the luxurious materials. The flannel pajamas were thick. He knew they would keep him warm during the rest of the winter. The pajama pants had a string around the waist, the top had long sleeves, and buttons started at the collar and went all the way down the front. The blue plaid button-up shirt fit him perfectly. It was a little long in the arms, but that just meant he could get more wear out of it.

"Are you children forgetting about your stockings?" Mother asked with a soft smile.

In the rush to finally open the wrapped presents, the children had indeed forgotten all about their stockings. Now they clambered toward the mantle.

George plunged his hand inside.

"A slingshot," he exclaimed as he pulled it out.

"Me, too!" Robert showed him. "I got a slingshot, too! Father, look! A slingshot!"

"You better thank your brothers for those," Father responded.

"Really?"

"Yes," said Mother. "They both sent a little extra money with this month's war salary and said to make sure all of you children got something for Christmas."

"What did you get?" George asked the girls.

They each held up a small bundle of white cloth and multicolored skeins of thread.

"Cross-stitch," said Eva proudly, "so we can start our very own needlework."

"Are your stockings empty?" Mother asked.

George shoved his hand to the toe and pulled out a large handful of wrapped chocolates.

"Is that all?" Mother asked, eyes still twinkling mischievously.

George turned his stocking inside out. But it was empty. He sat on the floor, admiring his presents. Pajamas, a shirt, a slingshot, and a small pile of chocolate. He figured he had to be the luckiest boy in the world this Christmas morning.

"Oh, dear me," said Mother with a grin. "I do believe I've forgotten one."

The children looked up at her, wondering how there could

possibly be even more presents on top of their already bountiful Christmas morning.

But she disappeared into her bedroom, emerging a moment later with another brown wrapped present.

"Who is that for?" asked Catherine.

"All of you," said Mother. "From the girls in Detroit."

She set the package in the middle of the floor, and the children tore the wrapping paper from the box.

"Oh, wow," said George, breathless, as the gift was uncovered.

"It's Monopoly!" Eva shouted. "Mother, they sent us Monopoly!"

"Yes," she laughed, "you best write to them and share your thanks. Or better yet, how about we go to Aunt Elvie's house after church and use her telephone to call them?"

The children all agreed.

"Now, hurry and go get dressed, or we'll be late for church. And we can't be late on Christmas morning," said Mother.

"Can we play just a little bit of Monopoly?" George pleaded.

"Not right now," she laughed, "but you can play when we return from church."

♦ ♦ ♦

The church sermon seemed to be the longest one that George had ever heard. He didn't know how it was possible to drone on and on about the same Bible verses. But today, the ministers seemed intent on keeping everyone in their pews for as long as possible.

George didn't comprehend a single word of what was being spoken. He was just dreaming of Monopoly.

After church, they phoned Aunt Doris and Uncle Roy's house in Detroit to wish the girls a merry Christmas and thank them for the gifts. The girls said they were doing well. All three had found jobs in the war factories and were very happy living in the city.

George saw Mother visibly gasp when the girls told her they rode the city bus to the factory every day, but they assured her there was nothing to worry about. Ann was working as a secretary, where she was responsible for keeping track of inventory for the military jeeps being produced. Elaine worked in the noisy factory, where she inspected shell casings for artillery rounds. Helena had taken to the hard work very quickly and was learning how to weld the tanks that were being made on the assembly line.

Their conversation on the phone was all too short. George could have talked to them for hours about the war materials being produced, especially the tanks. But eventually, Mother pulled them away from the phone, as they had to get home before the ham burned.

When they got home, the family feasted on a delicious Christmas ham dinner. As soon as dinner was done, the table cleared, the dishes washed, and the leftovers tucked away in the refrigerator, the children gathered around the table and played Monopoly for the rest of the day.

"Forget checkers," said George as he rolled doubles and

moved ten spaces. "I'll beat Albert and Taavi at Monopoly when they get back."

He held up a fistful of fake cash and looked at the properties lined up in front of him. He'd have to write a letter to each of his older brothers to thank them for the slingshot and tell them about the Monopoly game. A little part of him hoped they wouldn't have Monopoly at war so he could be sure to beat them when they came home. But then again, knowing how happy Monopoly made him, he also wished his brothers could be this happy, too.

19

I'm Flying!
January 1944

The middle of January brought weather so cold that the usually bustling streets of town remained nearly deserted. Deliverymen hurried about their days, braving the frigid air only out of necessity. Children skittered to and from the drafty brick schoolhouse. The schoolyard, where they usually congregated before and after classes, remained cold and empty. The air was bitter. The wind whipped. Snow fell unrelentingly from the sky, stacking in layers on top of layers like thick, down comforters.

George often wondered what winter was like for his brothers at war. If Albert was in southern Italy, he might be able to see snow on the far-off mountain peaks. Taavi had finished his training in Chicago and was now either in San Francisco or sailing west to the South Pacific. It was safe to say he was probably enjoying a nice, warm winter. George wished Taavi could bottle up some warmth and send it home, as the cold and snowy winters in northern Michigan were, at times, unbearable.

But the one good thing about the cold was it meant the Pine Street ice rink was in prime condition. Every day, after school was over, George quickly finished his chores so he could go there as soon as supper was finished. He bundled up in his heaviest winter clothing and walked through town to the ice rink.

A request for scorekeepers had gone out just after Christmas. George jumped at the opportunity. He moved from his usual game-watching perch in the bleachers and took up residence in the scorekeepers' box. The scorekeepers' box was right at center ice. It was sandwiched between the penalty boxes, which, in turn, were sandwiched between the players' benches.

"Goal for the Wolves," Rudy Mets said as he sat with George in the scorekeepers' box. "Number five, from numbers seventeen and twelve."

George took off his mitten, put a tally in the goal column next to Number 5's name, and marked an assist for 17 and 12. The Wolves were up, three to two, in the third period.

"How much time is left?" a burly hockey player asked as he skated toward center ice.

George looked at the stopwatch on the desk. "Four minutes, thirty-five seconds."

The desk, like most items at the ice rink, had been donated by a town resident. The lights hanging high over the ice were remnants from the public works department. The bleachers were wooden planks from the lumber yard, too warped to build any type of solid structure. The stopwatch was borrowed from the school gymnasium, though the gym teacher may not have known the "borrowing" had occurred.

"Glad this game is almost done," said Rudy from the chair next to George. "My hands are nearly icicles."

George rubbed his mittened hands together, breathing on

them in a feeble attempt to bring warmth to his fingers. Rudy did the same, but both boys still shivered. The bitter cold chewed through their heavy winter clothing with ease.

The seconds counted down on the stopwatch, and as the time turned over to zero, George put the silver whistle in his mouth and blew three shrill blasts.

The game was called to an end, and he heard the Jets players groan as a cheer erupted from the Wolves' bench.

Now that the last game of the night was finished, it was time to clean and prepare the ice so it would be ready for the next day. As the hockey players skated off the ice to remove their gear in the warming house that sat between the rink and Pine Street, George and Rudy, along with a dozen other boys, grabbed shovels and scraped the ice clean.

"Get the hose," Rudy called to George as they finished scraping the last of the rink.

George trudged behind the players' bench where a spigot emerged from the ground. A hose, connected to the spigot, was coiled in the snow. He grabbed the heavy rubber hose, a donated item from the local firehouse, and pulled it onto the rink. Then he turned the valve and let the water rush onto the ice.

Starting in the far corner, George coated the ice with a thin layer of water. It filled in the cracks and grooves from the day's skaters. By morning, it would be frozen smooth and solid, ready for a new day of hockey.

♦ ♦ ♦

One day, as George arrived home from school, he heard his neighbor across the street call out for him. He looked and saw Mr. Lindholm motioning for him to come over.

"Good afternoon, Mr. Lindholm," George said as he walked across the street.

"George, how are you?" the friendly neighbor asked.

George thought for a moment. He missed his sisters. He was worried about his brothers. School was monotonous. But all things considered, he couldn't complain, so he just said, "I'm fine, sir. And you?"

"Doing well, thank you. Now, do you have a moment to come inside? I have something you may like."

"I have to fill the woodbox for my mother, so I can't stay long."

"Won't take but a minute. Come on." Mr. Lindholm beckoned George inside. "Leave your boots on. It's cold down there."

He pointed to the stairs leading down to the cellar. He flicked the switch, illuminating the steps in dim, yellow light.

George followed after him, creaking down the wooden steps.

"Here," said Mr. Lindholm, reaching up to an overhead shelf. "I noticed you've been spending a lot of time at the ice rink and figure these probably fit you now. Care to try them on?"

George's jaw dropped. In Mr. Lindholm's hands was a pair of black ice skates.

"The boot is getting a little frayed at the toes, and the blades are a bit rusty. But I figure your Pa should have some bear grease to keep the frays at bay. And the rust on these blades is nothing a little shining and sharpening can't handle."

George couldn't speak. He couldn't believe the sight before him. He had wished and wished for a pair of hockey skates, and now that he was holding them, it seemed too good to be true.

"Here, sit." Mr. Lindholm pushed a stool toward George. "See if they fit."

George yanked off his boots. He pushed his feet into the skates, making sure the blades rested on a pile of old rags so he wouldn't chip them on the cement floor.

He laced them up over his ankles. They fit perfectly. Perhaps a little bit big, but he knew he'd be able to skate just fine.

"Oh, thank you, Mr. Lindholm," George said over and over again as he removed the skates and put his boots back on.

"You're welcome, George," his neighbor laughed. "I know things have been tough with your brothers gone and all. And I hear your sisters went south. Figured you'd get more use out of them than I would. I've just been watching them collect dust on the shelf for years."

"I will, sir. Thank you!"

George rushed home, his very own hockey skates held tightly in his hands.

"Mother, look!" he shouted as he ran inside. "Look what Mr. Lindholm gave me!"

"Ah, Yrjö, please take your boots off before you come into the kitchen."

George kicked his boots off and rushed back into the kitchen.

"Skates, Mother! He gave me ice skates!"

"What a wonderful gift," she said as she looked them over. "You better take good care of these. I hope you thanked him."

"Oh, I did. I promise. Maybe I could bring him some of Father's special cinnamon rolls from the bakery?"

"That would be a fine idea."

"But first, I must write to Ann. She said she would work hard in Detroit so she could buy me ice skates. But now, maybe she can buy her own pair instead."

George pulled a piece of paper and a pen from Mother's sewing basket and sat down at the kitchen table to tell Ann all about his new treasure.

That night, after supper, George brought Mr. Lindholm and his wife a platter of Father's fresh cinnamon rolls from the bakery. Then, he ran home and helped Father shine, polish, and sharpen his new skates. Once done, he ran as fast as he could down the street to the Pine Street ice rink.

The hockey games hadn't started yet for the evening, so the ice was open for anyone to use. He laced up his skates in the warming house and walked to the rink. He grabbed a hockey stick that was leaning in a snowbank and found a puck near the bleachers. He walked to the edge of the rink and hesitated for a moment as he looked out over the sheet of ice. Then, in one smooth stride, he stepped onto the ice. He glided for a bit and then began to push his feet outward just as he had watched the hockey players do.

He pushed and pushed, going faster and faster around the ice rink. The wind whistled past his ears. His eyes watered from the cold air. He felt weightless, as if he were soaring through the air.

I'm flying! George thought with a grin as he skated across the ice.

20

A Letter from Taavi
February 1944

George grabbed one last newspaper from the linen bag that hung across his shoulders. He glanced at it. The date printed on the top right corner read *Tiistai, 29 Helmikuu 1944*. Tuesday, February 29, 1944.

It was a leap year. He wouldn't see this date in February again for another four years. He wondered if he'd still be working at *The Suomi Times* on the next leap year. He had been delivering the Finnish newspaper every Tuesday and Thursday for the past five months. Rain or shine, hot or cold, the newspapers needed to be delivered. He had trudged through countless snowbanks, fended off dozens of stray dogs that nipped at his pant legs, and tossed paper after paper onto porches.

But all that hard work paid off when he got to payday. He heaved the last newspaper onto a porch and trudged through the cold to *The Suomi Times* printshop on Fifth Street.

"Hi, Gurney," George said to the printshop owner as he pushed the door open.

"Hiya, George. How was the walk today?"

"Same as usual," he shivered, taking off his wool mittens and breathing onto his hands in an attempt to warm them.

"Here's your pay," Gurney said as he took a handful of coins from a desk next to the printing press and gave them to George.

"Thanks," said George as he left the shop.

He tucked the money safely in his pocket and headed for home. Along the way, he stopped into Ruska's, the local restaurant. The warm air felt delightful as he sat on a high-topped stool at the counter and wriggled out of his coat. He unwound his scarf as Mr. Ruska welcomed him in.

"What can I get you today, young man?"

"Hot chocolate, please. Extra marshmallows."

"Coming right up," he said as he turned around to fill a mug with the steaming hot beverage. He scooped two mounds of marshmallows on top and pushed the mug across the table to George's shaking hands.

George put a five-cent piece on the counter, but Mr. Ruska shook his head.

"Today's your lucky day. Leap year comes but once in a while. This one's on the house."

George graciously sipped on the warm drink, thawing his hands by wrapping them around the white mug.

Once he was warm and satisfied with a belly full of hot chocolate, he said his thanks to Mr. Ruska, bundled up again, and went out into the cold. As he continued home, he stopped into the post office.

"Ready for the spring thaw?" the postmaster asked as George entered.

"Yes, sir. I'm ready for warmer weather but not ready to be

done skating for the year."

"I understand. But spring means baseball. I'm sure that'll be starting before you know it. Here's your mail," he said, handing it across the counter. "Looks like another letter from one of your brothers." The postmaster gave a small nod as George grabbed the letter and turned to leave. "Tell your folks I say hello."

"Will do," said George as he ran out the door and headed home.

He placed the letter and two dollars of his monthly earnings on the kitchen table for his mother. Then, he went upstairs to deposit his fifteen cents into the striped sock that doubled as his bank account. Inside was the crisp one-dollar bill from the fall potato harvest. He still wasn't sure what to spend it on. He usually spent the coins from his newspaper delivery earnings at Ruska's. But he still wasn't ready to part ways with the crisp dollar. He dropped the coins in. They jingled to the toe, and he closed the drawer.

"Thank you for the money." Mother hugged him as he came downstairs. "Ready to hear what Taavi has to say?"

The children gathered excitedly around Mother. Father sat in his recliner across the room, rocking back and forth.

Taavi began his letter by wishing the family well. He said he was fine. Training was finished, and he was scheduled to set sail on a brand-new destroyer. He said it was the finest of its kind, a beautiful, sturdy ship built so strongly that it couldn't sink even if all the sailors stood on one side and tried to overturn it. He was looking forward to watching some sunsets on the ship while sailing across the open ocean. Unlike the woodlands of home, where the tall pines and birch trees blocked the sunsets, the ocean was as vast and open as the eye could see, making for a wonderful view of the sky.

Mother paused in her reading to take a sip of her coffee.

George wondered about life on the ocean. He knew from school that the Pacific was the largest ocean. It wrapped all the way around the globe that sat on his teacher's desk. He wondered how long it would take to sail across it and where exactly Taavi was heading. Before he left, Taavi said he might end up in the South Pacific, but he wasn't certain. George thought maybe he would even end up in Japan, or perhaps one of the small refueling islands between the United States and the Far East lands.

Taavi finished his letter by describing the scenery in San Francisco.

The water here is so salty. It's nothing like the freshwater lakes back home. Even spray from the wind as it blows waves against the rocks tastes salty. The beaches are sandy, much like at home. Seaweed washes onto them in large clumps. And lots of sea creatures like crabs and shellfish get tangled up and deposited onto the shore. I suppose by the time you get this, I'll be halfway around the world surrounded by an ocean of deep blue. I love you all, and I can't wait to be home soon.

Signed,

Taavi.

♦ ♦ ♦

George sat in the back of Ms. Johansson's class the next day. As she droned on about long division and the importance of carrying the remainder, he gazed at the world map. According to Albert's last letter, he was still in southern Italy. The Allies were trying to push the Axis powers out of the country. Taavi was somewhere in the vast ocean of blue on the left side of the map, sailing on a brand-new ship across the Pacific. George never dreamed he would be so far away from his brothers, each one on opposite sides of the world, facing dangers that he couldn't even imagine.

Suddenly, George was yanked from his daydreams by the shrill air raid sirens that screamed through the school, demanding the children take cover.

"Under your desks," Ms. Johansson said as she marched up and down the aisles to make sure the students were safely tucked beneath them.

George pulled his feet in as far as he could. The sirens continued their piercing cries. He crouched for many minutes, waiting for the terrible ruckus to quiet down. Air raid drills were a normal part of their lessons, and he heard them at least once a week. Still, the sirens always sent chills down his spine. They made the war seem very real and very close to home.

At last, the sirens faded and made way for the all-clear signal. The children crawled out from under their desks. Ms. Johansson resumed her lesson on long division, and George was left to worry about his brothers, the siren ringing in his daydreams and thoughts of war swirling in his mind.

♦ ♦ ♦

As the day ended, George completed his usual routine of chores and supper before heading to the ice rink to skate. He went with John today, even though John didn't have any skates. Will was also supposed to meet them there, and the boys were going to take turns using George's skates.

"You might want two pairs of socks." George pulled an extra set of wool socks from his coat pocket. "Eva gave me these. They help prevent blisters since the skates are a bit big."

John pulled the navy blue socks over the pair that was already on his feet and laced up the skates.

"How do you make it look so easy?" he asked George.

"Just watch the hockey players and copy their movements," said George. "It's more of a push outward movement instead of a step forward. And make sure to bend your knees and lean a little bit forward. It'll help you go faster."

John tried his best to listen to George's advice. He made two slow laps around the ice rink before sitting down to take the skates off.

"I don't know how you do it," he said as he undid the laces.

"Let me try," said Will, who had finally arrived.

The boys sat back as Will put on the extra pair of socks and laced up the skates.

"Never done this before," he said as he flashed a grin. "Wish me luck."

Before George and John could answer, Will stepped onto the ice, took one timid step, and fell in a spectacular blur of arms, legs, and skates.

"Ugh," he groaned and pulled himself to a sitting position.

George and John burst out laughing, asking through the giggles if Will was all right.

"A bruised ego, but that should heal as soon as I get these skates off. Looks like Old Man Lindholm knew what he was doing when he gave them to you," Will said as he gave the skates back to George.

The boys watched open skate for a while, then George went into the warming house to suit up. He had been invited to join a hockey team a few weeks back and had enjoyed playing the fast games. Every day, he got a little better. It took a lot of practice, but he enjoyed every minute spent on the ice.

As George's game started, he realized they were playing Ricky McClain's team. He avoided Ricky during the school days, but since they were both forwards on opposing teams, it would be impossible to steer clear of him tonight.

"What dumpster did you pull those rags out of?" Ricky sneered and tapped George's skates with his hockey stick as they lined up for the faceoff.

"Not telling you," George replied. "Otherwise, you'll try to get a pair for yourself."

The puck dropped, and George took off past Ricky. He soared around the ice, connecting play after play with his teammates. By the end of the game, they were winning, three to zero. As he skated back to the warming house, he purposely passed by Ricky, who was sitting on his team's bench.

"If you ask nicely," George said with a grin, "I'll tell you the best dumpster to find skates. Maybe then, you could keep up."

Ricky glared.

George knew he shouldn't gloat, and Mother would scold him if she found out, but it felt good to win against Ricky and wipe the smug smile off his face, even if just for a little while.

21

Big Fat Eggs
April 1944

"Mother," George croaked as he hobbled into the kitchen, "I don't feel good."

George's mother looked up from the pot of oatmeal she was stirring, a line of worry creased between her eyes.

"Oh, no," she said and hurried across the room. "What's wrong, Yrjö?"

"I feel like I have big, fat eggs in my neck."

She felt his neck and placed a hand on his forehead.

"Oh, dear," she murmured. "I was worried this would happen. I'm afraid you have the mumps. It's been running rampant through town. You better head back up to bed."

George could hardly make it up the stairs. His legs were weak. His head was pounding in pain. And his throat was so swollen he could barely swallow. Mother helped him up the last few steps and back into bed.

"And how are you feeling, Robert?" she asked George's younger brother who still lay in bed.

"Hot and aching," he moaned.

"Does your throat hurt?"

"Not right now. But I have a headache."

"Get some rest. It looks like you'll be home from school for a while. I'll go check on the girls."

George heard his mother enter his sisters' bedroom. She closed the door a few minutes later. There weren't any footsteps following her downstairs, so George knew they were all sick, too.

He tossed and turned in bed. First, he was so cold that he pulled the blankets up tight and shivered underneath. Then, in what felt like a matter of minutes, he was sweating and had to kick all the covers to the foot of the bed. And, just as suddenly, he was shivering again and huddled under the blankets. The process continued over and over.

Mother came into the room, offering them cold water and warm broth.

"I've called for Dr. Sheffield," she said. "He'll come by during his afternoon rounds."

She pressed her hand to George's forehead. "I'm afraid your fever is just getting worse. I'll go chill some washcloths in the refrigerator."

All morning long, Mother bustled between the two bedrooms. She brought cold compresses, refilled broth bowls, and made sure all the children were drinking plenty of water. George didn't feel like eating or drinking anything, but he obeyed Mother's instructions as best possible.

"I remember having the mumps when I was a little girl," she told the boys during one trip to their room. "I'm sorry, I know how miserable it is."

Dr. Sheffield came in the afternoon.

"Open, please," he ordered George as he performed an examination.

George opened his mouth even though the pain radiated down his throat.

"Yes, you all have a healthy case of the mumps," Dr. Sheffield said. "I'm afraid you'll just have to rest this one out. I gave your mother a bottle of tonic to help ease the aches and pains. It won't make the mumps go away any faster, but in the meantime, it should make you feel a little better."

George rolled over after the doctor left, groaning in pain. He'd never felt anything like it and wished the mumps would go away soon. He thought back to the day the honey dippers came last October to empty and clean their outhouse. Cruz, the older of the two honey dippers, told George he had been cleaning outhouses ever since he was a little boy, and he never got sick. He said the smell scared the germs away.

George thought Cruz was the luckiest man in the world. George decided he'd empty every single outhouse in town if it meant he wouldn't have to deal with the mumps.

♦ ♦ ♦

A week and a half passed with George and his siblings bedridden. The days were long and the nights were restless. But slowly, their bodies fought off the mumps. One by one, they crawled out of bed and went downstairs. Mother fed them hearty stew and freshly baked bread. They were all weak with fatigue, having not eaten a true meal in over ten days.

"Eat your stew, Yrjö," Mother said as she ruffled his hair. "It'll do your body good to get some nourishment."

George ate what he could. Even though he was hungry, his stomach wasn't used to the large quantity of food, and he could only finish half of what was in his bowl. Then, he curled up in Father's recliner and listened to the radio. He had missed almost two weeks of news, so it felt good to get caught up with the latest war progress. The Allies had bombed Romania and Eastern Europe quite heavily. The Japanese were retreating in Burma. Although both were deemed victories for the Allies, the advances came at a heavy loss of Allied life.

Once he got enough strength back, George knew he would have to mark the progress on Taavi's map. And he'd also have to find Romania in Europe and Burma in Asia, since he couldn't remember where those countries were located. But right now, he was too tired to walk across the yard to the barn.

He switched between the war updates and a Western program that told a story of a train and its passengers being held hostage by a group of bandits in the Wild West. As he caught the tail end of one of the war broadcasts, he grinned as he heard the Detroit Tigers baseball season was starting up again. He liked listening to the Tigers games almost as much as he enjoyed listening to the Red Wings. Nothing could outrank hockey, but if anything was going to come close, it was baseball.

He felt like he was emerging from a long winter's hibernation as he healed from the mumps. The sun had come out from its winter hiding place behind the snowy clouds. With the reappearance of the sun came warmer weather. The Pine Street ice rink had melted away, or at least that's what Father told him one day when he came home from work. It was now the middle of April, and of course, that meant the baseball season would be starting soon. George just couldn't believe how quickly it had snuck up on him.

His body still ached, and his throat wasn't totally healed yet, so he spent a few more days curled up in Father's recliner. He enjoyed the quiet afternoons with his mother when his siblings were at school. The girls said they felt healthy enough, so they had gone back to school. Even Robert joined them. George was in no rush to get back to school, so he told Mother he needed a few more days of rest before heading back. Maybe after the weekend.

"It's not fair," Eva pouted as she came home from school one afternoon.

"What's not fair?" Mother asked.

"George gets to stay home all day. The mumps are gone. They even took our quarantine sign off the window."

"I'm still tired," George said, though he knew he was more than well enough to go back to school.

"Don't worry about your brother," Mother warned Eva. "He will return to school when he's ready. He still seems a little under the weather. Just be grateful you healed so quickly and can go back to school. Some children are left with lifelong complications from the mumps. Let's hope George doesn't face any such challenges. You let him rest."

George grinned at Eva behind Mother's back and turned the volume up a couple of notches on the radio so he could hear the Tigers game easier. She rolled her eyes and stomped upstairs.

"Come on, come on," George said to himself. It was the bottom of the third inning, and the Tigers were losing five to nothing. Runners were on second and third. George held his breath as the pitch was delivered.

Crack! He heard the bat hit the ball and the announcer called the play. The runners at second and third advanced to home. The batter was safe at first.

"Yes!" George pumped his fist. "Yes! Come on, boys, you've got this!"

"See, Mother?" Eva peered through the banister. "He's fine."

A sheepish grin stretched across George's face. Mother looked at him as she kneaded bread dough in the kitchen.

"Yes, I agree, Eva. He seems to be better." Her voice was firm, but she had a twinkle in her eyes. "You can go to school with your siblings tomorrow."

22

Spring at Last
April 1944

All but the tallest snowbanks were melted by the time George went back to school. Mother said there had been a late spring snowstorm a week ago, but he had been too sick to notice.

Now, the sun shone bright, bringing the earth back to life from its long winter slumber. Buds were on the trees, and soon the little green leaves would unravel to collect the summer sunshine.

The Allies continued to make headway in the war, and George was optimistic that this spring was going to bring good times ahead.

"Got your glove?" John asked as the boys met on the street in front of their houses.

"Right here," George said, having just pulled the baseball glove from his closet earlier that morning.

"Great. Let's go. I bet they're getting ready to start."

The boys headed away from town, past the lumber mill, to the baseball fields on the other side of the highway. The infields were still a muddy mess. The grass in the outfields was brown and pocketed with puddles of melted snow. But excitement filled the fresh spring air. It was their very first day of baseball games for the season, and a little mud wasn't going to spoil the fun.

All the boys from George's seventh-grade class were there, along with the sixth and eighth graders. There were six baseball fields, each one filled with boys warming up for the day.

"Over there." John pointed to his and George's waiting teammates.

"'Bout time!" Cliff Beasley tossed the ball to George as they jogged over. "First pitch is in five minutes. Do you boys still want to play first and center?"

"You betcha," John said as he jogged to the center of the outfield.

George fired the ball back to Cliff and took his position on first base.

"Toss me a few," he told Cliff, who stood on the pitcher's mound.

George took a few warm-up tosses and rolled his shoulder and arm in circles to loosen the joints.

"Play ball!" came a cry from the other bench.

A batter stood in position, bat readied over his shoulder. Cliff threw a zinger right down the middle of the plate.

Strike!

The boys in the field cheered.

Cliff threw another one.

Strike!

More whoops and cheering from the outfield.

"Better brush off that rust, boys!" John jeered to the other team. "Come on, give us something to run after!"

The third pitch left Cliff's hand. The batter eyed it up, swung, and connected. *Crack!*

George smiled at the glorious sound of the bat hitting the ball. Spring had officially arrived! He watched as the ball sailed in a high arc over the infield. John sprinted after it, glove extended. As the ball neared the end of its trajectory, he reached, stretched, and dove. He hit the soggy ground nearly horizontal, and mud flew into the air as he slid.

"You're out!" John shouted with glee as he hopped to his feet, ball securely caught in his glove, mud dripping from head to toe.

George and his teammates cheered, ready for the next batter.

◆ ◆ ◆

By the end of the day, every single boy was a muddy and soggy mess. George's body ached. His shoulder was sore. The palms of his hands were stinging from countless at-bats and catches. His clothes were filthy. But George and John were filled with joy as they walked home.

"Four and two," John said as he skipped along next to George. "We're off to a good start this season."

"And that was without Red Dog," said George. "His mumps should be gone in a week. He's our best batter by far. Once he gets back in the lineup, we should be able to get some decent RBIs."

The boys' shoes sloshed as they ran across the highway toward home.

"Do you think the dam is open so we can clean up in the

water?" George asked.

"Should be. My pa caught a trout there last weekend. And I know Ma will tan my hide if I come home looking like this."

"Same," George agreed.

The boys took a path around the lumber yard, over the railroad tracks, and behind their street to the swimming hole at the dam.

"I don't know about this," John said, pushing an ice chunk from the shore with his shoe.

"Just go quick," George said, placing his glove on a small patch of snow under a pine tree.

The boys shrieked and laughed as they plunged into the icy water, clothes and all. The water was so cold it squeezed the air right out of George's chest as he dove under.

"Too bad we don't have any soap," George said as he splashed the frigid water on his face and scrubbed his skin clean.

"Dunno," said John through chattering teeth. "I don't think I could stay in here any longer to wash soap out of my hair."

The boys, now clean enough to be able to show up at home without getting a scolding, stripped down to their underclothes and dashed through the forest. They hung their pants and shirts on the clothesline in George's backyard and headed to their respective houses.

"See you tomorrow," George called.

"Want to go fishing after church?" asked John.

George agreed, then ran inside to get into his pajamas while he waited for his clothes to dry in the warm spring breeze.

It was nearly suppertime when a knock on the back door alerted the family to a visitor. It was Will, with his weekly egg delivery.

"Sorry I'm late, ma'am," George heard him say as he handed the crate of eggs to Mother. "This mud is thicker'n a tub full of honey. Had the worst time getting the truck out of the barnyard."

"Can you stay for supper?"

George held his breath, fingers crossed.

"I suppose I should finish my route, ma'am."

George felt his chest deflate. He hadn't seen Will in a while and wanted to spend some time with him.

"But," Will continued, "I can get this egg route done in thirty minutes flat and then be back—if you don't mind holding a plate for me."

"Not at all. Run along now," Mother encouraged him.

George ran to the clothesline in the backyard to grab his pants and shirt that were now dry from the warm sunshine. He changed out of his pajamas, then set up the Monopoly board on the floor next to the fireplace in preparation for Will's visit.

After supper was finished, the dishes cleared, and the evening chores completed, George and Will played Monopoly long into the evening. They listened to the radio as it brought news of the war and entertaining programs into the house.

"Want to go fishing with me and John tomorrow?" George asked as they finished their game.

"What time and where?"

"After church, to the fishing log down the river a ways.

Follow the old bear path north from the dam, and you can't miss it. It's the huge oak tree that fell across the water a few years back."

"I'll be there."

♦ ♦ ♦

The boys spent the next afternoon wrestling fish from the raging river. The melting snow had caused the banks to swell so much that they couldn't even sit on their fishing log. Instead, they rolled up their pants and cast their lines in from the bank.

They trudged home many hours later, bucket laden with fish.

"Wow, Yrjö, there's enough for a few meals here," Father said as he looked down at George's portion of the catch.

"Yes, sir. The bigger the rapids, the bigger the fish. At least that's what Old Widower Robinson taught Will."

"Robinson is a wise man. Now, do you think we should fry these up for supper?"

George agreed, then grabbed an armful of logs from the woodpile and filled the woodbox. He stoked the woodstove and placed a skillet on top to heat. Then he went back outside to help Father clean the fish.

23

School Picnic
April 1944

It was the last Saturday in April and a day of celebration for all the children in school. That's because it was the annual spring picnic, a day where all the families came together on the school grounds to eat, visit, and play. The sun was shining, and the grass had gained a tremendous amount of green coloring in the past two weeks.

"May I please carry the picnic basket?" Eva asked Mother.

"Certainly, but make sure you don't skip. I don't want the sandwiches to get smashed."

"I'm fourteen now, and much too old to skip," Eva reminded Mother of her recently passed birthday.

"Then I'm sure we will enjoy perfectly intact sandwiches come lunchtime."

George and Robert ran ahead of their family to claim a picnic spot. The school grounds were already abuzz with students and their families. George found a place for their blanket next to a large oak tree and smoothed the wrinkles from the fabric as he spread it on the ground.

"What a perfect spot," Mother commented as the rest of the family joined.

"Look, the races are already starting!" George pointed,

tugging on Mother's sleeve.

"Run along, boys," she said. "We'll stay here and set out the lunch. Don't be gone too long. After we eat, you'll have the whole afternoon to play."

George and Robert took off through the field, running down the small hill to the football field where the footraces were about to begin.

"There's your class." George nudged Robert in the direction of his teacher. "I'll meet up with you after."

He joined the rest of the seventh graders as they huddled together and waited for their turn to race. The races started with the youngest grades and worked to the older children. First, the girls in each grade raced, then, the boys.

One teacher would call the next group to the end zone while two more teachers helped make sure no one was getting a head start by placing their toes over the goal line. Once the runners were in position, one of the teachers blew a shrill blast on a whistle, and the children took off down the field.

George's heart pounded faster and faster in his chest as his turn neared. The seventh-grade girls were now in position. The whistle blew and they took off down the field. George heard the seventh-grade boys being called to the starting line and took a step forward to place his toe on the white line of the end zone.

"On your mark," the teacher bellowed.

George crouched.

"Get set."

He shifted his weight to his front leg.

The whistle blew. George lunged forward. He pumped his arms. His legs carried him so fast he felt like he was flying across the grass. Closer and closer to the finish line at the opposing end zone. In his peripherals, he could see that some of his classmates were neck and neck with him. His lungs burned, but still, he pushed faster, taking the longest strides he could. With one last leap, he charged over the finish line and turned to look at the field.

Crossing the finish line at almost the exact same time was Cliff Beasley, the pitcher on George's baseball team.

They both looked at the teacher who was judging the races.

"First place goes to you, young man." He smiled and walked toward George, handing him a blue ribbon. "Congratulations. It was a close call."

"Aw, man." Cliff clutched his ribs, evidence of a cramp settling into his muscles. "Could have beat you if not for this stitch."

"Excuses, excuses," said George with a grin. "Looks like you're better suited for the pitching mound instead of the track-and-field team."

George walked off the field, blue ribbon clutched in his hand. He passed Ricky McClain. George held his tongue, though he would have liked to rub it in Ricky's face that money couldn't buy everything, not even a first-place ribbon. Some things had to be won through hard work.

◆ ◆ ◆

After the races, George rejoined his family on the blanket under the oak tree.

"Good job, George," Mother said while his sisters showered him with praise.

Beaming at the compliments, George said, "In our next letter to Albert and Taavi, I'll have to tell them I won."

"I'm sure they'd love to hear." Mother squeezed his shoulders.

The family dug into the picnic basket that Mother had packed full of sandwiches, fruit tarts, peanuts, and buttered biscuits drizzled with honey. George couldn't think of a better way to spend the day. He lay back on the blanket as the rest of the family finished their lunch.

"Shall we get some ice cream?" George's father asked.

George and Robert hopped up.

"What kind do you all want?" George asked Mother and his sisters.

A chorus of orders filled the air as they requested an assortment of chocolate, vanilla, and strawberry.

Father, George, and Robert walked across the field and down a short path through the woods that led to a large white tent where the ice cream was being served.

As they crunched across the gravel, a commotion off the path to his left caught George's attention. Ricky McClain cowered against a tree. His father towered over him with his voice and fist raised in anger. George couldn't hear what Ricky's father was saying, but the tone of his loud voice carried through the trees.

The scene had now garnered the attention of Father and Robert, and they slowed to watch in shocked silence as Ricky's father wound up and hurled his ice cream. It smashed into the tree above Ricky's head, white ice cream splattering onto the brown tree trunk and dripping into Ricky's hair.

"Let's go," Robert whimpered, tugging at Father's sleeve.

George looked at Ricky's fear-filled face. Specks of melted ice cream matted his hair. His body was shrunk as low as possible to the ground, hands raised in a weak attempt to cover his face.

George didn't like Ricky in the least bit. He was relentless in his teasing. He made fun of George every chance he got and taunted him that his brothers were likely to die in war simply for being poor. He was mean, nasty, and always picked on anyone he could get his hands on.

But it still hurt to see Ricky being treated like a helpless, cornered animal.

"Father?" asked George.

"I'll handle it. You go on, get the ice cream, and bring it back to your mother and sisters."

Father gave them each a nudge and stepped from the path to address the situation. George and Robert looked over their shoulders as they slowly walked away. They saw Father grab Mr. McClain by the collar and haul him down the street and out of sight.

Ricky glanced at George, and for a brief moment, a glimpse of something resembling gratefulness filled his eyes. Then, he scampered back to the field in search of his own mother, rubbing the melted ice cream from his hair.

George wondered what could possibly make a man act so angry on such a beautiful picnic day.

Father returned after the ice cream had been eaten and the family was in various states of relaxation on the picnic blanket. Robert had already spilled the beans on Ricky's father being marched out of the picnic.

"Is it true that Mr. McClain lost his marbles?" Mary asked Father loudly.

"Robert said he was acting like a madman," added Eva.

"Shh," Mother hushed the girls. "Solomon, what happened?"

"Seems McClain stopped by the tavern on his way over and indulged a bit too much. But let's not worry, children. It's all taken care of. He's home now and won't disrupt our picnic anymore."

George rolled over on the blanket, full of ice cream and enjoying the warm sunshine on his face.

After a while, he heard the call go out that it was time for more games. All afternoon, he and his classmates participated in the games and contests. They played capture the flag, kick the can, hopscotch, double Dutch, and more. There were prizes for contests in the baseball toss, farthest football punt, three-legged race, wheelbarrow race, sack race, and many others.

George ended the picnic with a third-place ribbon, two second-place ribbons, and his blue first-place ribbon from the footrace. His brother and sisters all had their share of ribbons as well. They laughed and joked all the way home as afternoon faded into evening.

As soon as they got home, George went into the barn and pinned his ribbons up on the wall above Taavi's workbench. He couldn't wait to show his brothers what he had won. He knew they would be pleased. Perhaps they would even bring home their own medals and awards from war.

♦ ♦ ♦

George ran inside the house to clean his hands and face before joining the family for a quick supper. Now that the sun was keeping the sky bright late into the evening, George and Robert had time after their chores were finished to toss a baseball back and forth in the yard.

"Hold it a little more on top of the seam with your middle finger," George instructed. "Now, really snap your middle finger down when you release."

Robert threw the ball. It landed squarely in George's glove with a thud.

"Not bad," George said. "You're getting the hang of it."

"It's hard to get the curve."

"Taavi will have to show you when he gets back. He throws the nastiest curveballs. I can never get them quite as good as he does, but that's the gist of it."

The boys tossed the ball back and forth, practicing curveballs, fastballs, and tossing it high into the sky to practice catching pop flies.

As they went inside to enjoy another night of checkers, they turned on the radio to a replay of the Detroit Tigers and Cleveland Indians baseball game. The game had taken place during the day, but the boys had been at the picnic and unable to catch the live broadcast. Instead, they listened to the evening replay, cheering when the Tigers scored and urging them on as they fell behind.

Ultimately, the Tigers lost another one, and the boys retired to bed, a little disappointed in the performance of their beloved baseball team.

As always, George thought of his brothers as he drifted off to sleep. Albert was probably getting ready to wake up soon in some faraway European land. It was already tomorrow there.

And Taavi would be enjoying the evening, watching the sun set in front of him as he sailed across the Pacific Ocean on a destroyer bound for a distant shore.

George ran his fingers over Taavi's pencil that he kept in his pocket, always ready to update the map on his workbench with the Allies' progress in the war. He hoped that his brothers would be able to come home soon. Then, they could have a big checkers tournament, and he could show them how much better he had gotten in the past few months.

24

The Blackest Night
May 1944

"I'll buy it," George said triumphantly as he counted out six spaces and landed on Boardwalk.

"Not fair!" said Robert. "Now you can put hotels on the blue ones, and you already have the purple group."

"Should've bought it when you had the chance," George said as he handed his four hundred dollars to Eva, the banker of their board game.

The five children were upstairs in the girls' bedroom playing a game of Monopoly. The wet Saturday weather was keeping them indoors. The rain whipped in horizontal sheets against the windows, and wind tugged at the shutters.

George glanced outside, hoping the clouds would clear soon. But a thick blanket of black covered the sky, indicating no end in sight to the angry rain. He snuggled under the quilt as he collected the Boardwalk card, grateful to be inside the cozy house.

"I got doubles," Catherine said gleefully, moving her piece out of jail.

"My turn," said Mary as she rolled the dice across the board.

The metal game pieces moved around and around the board as the children played into the afternoon.

A gust of wind tore at the house, and George shivered as he glanced out the second-story bedroom window. This was the first major storm they had been hit with all spring. It was nothing like the soft snowfalls of winter. The ominous thunderheads boiled across the sky, bubbling and foaming as they continued to release a torrent of rain.

A lightning bolt flashed across the sky, the subsequent crack of thunder so loud it caused the children to jump. Robert cowered next to Mary, who put an arm around him.

"Don't worry," she soothed him. "It'll pass soon."

Another bolt of lightning lit up the room. Thunder followed in close pursuit, rolling across the dark sky.

Then, the wind changed. The rain seemed to hesitate. A sudden and thick silence blanketed the room.

Eva paused mid-roll.

The children glanced at each other.

Catherine was the first to rise.

"Something isn't right," she said.

George agreed. An eerie calm had descended upon the house. One after another, the children silently descended the stairs to the living room below.

Father was reading the newspaper. Mother was knitting in her rocking chair.

"What's wrong?" she asked as five wide-eyed children stood in a line at the bottom of the steps.

Knock, knock, knock.

It came from the front door. Company never came to the

front door. They always knew to go around to the back entryway. Front doors were just a formality in their close-knit community. Even the deliverymen used the back door.

George knew of only one man who knocked on front doors.

His stomach churned. His feet were as heavy as lead blocks. His mouth felt like he had been gnawing on a handful of cotton balls.

He took a few hesitant steps toward the door, willing time to stop so he didn't have to answer it.

Knock, knock, knock.

He reached a hand out, grasping the cold metal knob. The door stuck for a moment, then scraped across the wood floor.

There he stood. The Western Union man. Silhouetted in the rain. Hat askew from the wind. Holding a small slip of paper.

He didn't say a word. He just handed the paper to George, then turned and vanished into the dark and stormy afternoon.

"Yrjö?" Mother's small voice questioned from her rocking chair.

"It's—it's a telegram," he whispered.

No one spoke.

Catherine moved closer to George. She placed her hand on his shoulder.

"Please, can you read it?" Mother asked, her voice shaking, face pale.

George slipped the envelope open. Inside was a single-sided card. The words "Western Union" were stamped in bold letters across the top. Under that, the short letter was addressed to

George's mother.

George's throat tightened as he scanned the words. He didn't want to read them out loud. He wanted to run after the Western Union man, give the card back, and tell him to make it not true.

"What does it say, Yrjö?" Father asked softly.

He cleared his throat, holding back tears.

"The Secretary of War desires me to express his deep regret that your son Taavi was killed in action on twenty-nine April 1944 in the South Pacific. Buried at sea."

Mother was the first to burst into sobs. "No. No, oh please, no. Please, it can't be true. No, no, no," she pleaded with an upturned face.

George fell to his knees on the wood floor, his legs unable to hold him upright. Great sobs escaped his chest and tears poured from his eyes. He clutched the telegram in his shaking hands, gripping it tightly while simultaneously wanting to rip it to shreds.

It was Taavi. Taavi was gone.

He rubbed his fists across his face in a futile attempt to dry his eyes. It was useless. The tears wouldn't stop. He glanced across the room, his vision now blurred from the tears. His sisters clutched each other, great cries shaking their bodies. Father moved from his recliner to pull Mother into an embrace. Robert latched onto Mother's skirt, hiding his tears from view.

Taavi was gone.

The ache in George's chest was so fierce, he didn't know it was possible to feel such pain.

A sheet of rain lashed at the windows. George leaned against the wall and pulled himself up, knees weak with grief. He placed the telegram facedown on the kitchen table. He didn't want to see it anymore. No one needed to read those cruel words.

The family gathered around one another. No one was able to offer any type of comfort other than letting each other cry out in anguish.

George thought back to the day they went to the train station to send Taavi off. As hard as it was to worry about both of his brothers away fighting in the war, the unknown version of war was better. The waiting was hard, the wondering caused plenty of anxiety, but it hurt less. It hurt less than the knowledge of this finality of war. The knowledge that he would never get to see his brother again.

He thought of his last goodbye to Taavi. If only he could return to that moment. Pause time. Beg Taavi, like Mother had, to stay working in the copper mines instead of going to war. George would have done anything to change that day, to make it different. To make sure that Taavi never got on that train to go to war.

Finally, Father broke the silence. "I'll go to Elvie's to phone the girls in Detroit."

Mother nodded, a white handkerchief clutched to her red, swollen face.

Father disappeared into the rain, walking the few short blocks to Aunt Elvie's house to use her telephone.

George curled up in Father's recliner, eyes glazed over with tearful grief. *Your son Taavi was killed in action on twenty-nine April 1944.*

April twenty-ninth. He focused on that. April twenty-ninth was one week prior. The day of the school picnic. When George had won his first-place ribbon. The sky had been a beautiful, cloudless blue. The family had spent the day laughing and playing with their friends and classmates. They had been completely oblivious to the heartbreak and devastation that had happened halfway around the world, somewhere in that ocean of blue.

Twenty-nine April 1944. South Pacific. Buried at sea. Buried at sea. Buried at sea. George couldn't get the image out of his head. He knew it happened. He heard it on the war broadcasts all the time. Buried at sea. For some reason, when the radio broadcaster said those words, they didn't sound so cruel. Just a necessity of war. But seeing them printed in black ink on the telegram next to his own brother's name made them infinitely more painful.

George's father returned, wiping a mixture of raindrops and tears from his face.

"Roy and Doris will head north in the morning with the girls," he said, eyes bleak and voice lifeless. "Elvie was going to phone the minister to discuss the service details."

"What about Albert?" George whispered to Father.

"He will be notified by his superiors. But we will also write a letter and send him our love."

"Is he going to be safe?"

"Ah, Yrjö, we can only ask the Good Lord to watch over him. We don't know what the future of the war will bring. But we can hope and pray that Albert will come home in due time."

George pushed his face into the worn fabric of Father's

recliner, hiding his tears. He didn't like Father's answer, but he knew it wasn't Father's fault that the war didn't care who lived or died.

It didn't take long for the tragic news to spread through the town. The house began to fill with mourners. Friends and family, neighbors and shopkeepers, teachers, and even some people whom George had never met stopped by to offer their condolences to the family.

John came by to comfort his friend. He sat on the wood floor next to George. Neither boy spoke. There were no words to be had.

Someone brought over a box of hymn books from the church. Soft melodies filled the home in an attempt to bring comfort when such comfort was impossible to find.

Safe in the arms of Jesus
Safe on his gentle breast
There, by his love o'ershaded
Sweetly my soul shall rest

George didn't want Taavi safe in the arms of Jesus. He wanted him here. Home. Safe with the family.

♦ ♦ ♦

Long into the night, visitors continued to show up. Some offered a quick hug or a handshake and then hurried on their way. Many stayed to offer comfort. They sang when their voices would allow and cried with and consoled the family when they would not.

And everyone brought food. So much food. As if the hole in their hearts could be filled by such sustenance. The counters were overflowing with plates and baskets. The table was piled high with breads and jams and jars of preserved meats and vegetables.

George's fingers traced patterns in the fabric of Father's recliner. Strong hands squeezed his shoulders. Ladies kissed him on the forehead. A baby cried out in hunger, oblivious to the heartbreak going on around it.

No one slept in their beds that night. Mother didn't even mention bedtime. They huddled in the living room in various states of sleep as the guests made sure they were never left alone. At one point, someone carried Robert to Mother and Father's bed. John got called home by his own mother.

Finally, George was carried into his parents' bed and tucked under the blankets with Robert. Catherine curled up next to him. Sleep tugged at his eyelids, but his mind wouldn't submit to the command.

He missed Taavi. And he'd give anything to be able to see him one last time.

25

The Blackest Day
May 1944

It had been two days since George's family had received the awful telegram sharing the news of Taavi's death. Two days of grieving. Crying. Begging for it not to be true. The girls from Detroit arrived late Sunday night, awakening a whole new round of tears.

Now it was Monday. George should have been walking to school with his siblings. But instead, he was walking to the church for the funeral service.

There would be no casket. No body to be viewed. *Buried at sea.* Perhaps that was the cruelest trick of the whole nightmare. They just had to believe Taavi wasn't coming home.

The church was nearly empty when they arrived. Aunt Elvie was at the front of the sanctuary organizing flower arrangements. The photograph that had been taken before Taavi's departure was propped up on a small table. He stood tall, flanked on either side by Mother and Father, a smile pulling at the corners of his mouth as he tried to be serious.

The door on the side of the church opened, and more flower arrangements were carried in. The minister entered from his study at the back of the church.

"Solomon, Aina," he said, shaking their hands, "you have my

deepest sympathies."

Father nodded. Mother dabbed her eyes with a handkerchief.

The minister then shook each of the children's hands, offering condolences.

George sat in the front pew with the younger of his siblings. The older sisters stood near the front of the church to welcome guests and accept the sympathies offered. Soon, funeral guests flooded the sanctuary. Hymns from the pipe organ filled the air.

Robert sniffled next to George, face buried in his hands.

As the line of mourners cycled through and found seats for the service, George glanced back. The church was filled with guests. Many of the faces he recognized. Some he did not. It didn't matter. He was glad the church was full. It comforted him slightly to be surrounded by so many people and to know that Taavi was loved and remembered by more than just him.

He felt a tap on his shoulder and turned to look. Will was there, tears streaming down his cheeks as his small frame was dwarfed by a suit coat made for a grown man.

Will didn't say anything. He hugged George tightly, then sat down in the pew and wiped his eyes on the gigantic coat sleeve that George could only guess had been pulled from Old Widower Robinson's closet.

George rubbed his eyes with a handkerchief that Mary had loaned him, sniffling as the tears fell. He was glad his friend was sitting next to him.

"War is dumb," Will whispered through hiccupped sobs. "Taavi didn't deserve none of this. It wasn't his war. But he was so strong and brave, that he still volunteered to fight. I'm sorry you lost your brother because of all this."

"And I'm sorry you lost your family, too," George said, realizing he now had a lot more in common with Will. Losing family members, whether through death or being sent away on an orphan train, wasn't easy on anyone.

The minister called the congregation to attention in prayer. George and Will bowed their heads.

"In the name of the Father, and of the Son, and of the Holy Ghost. Amen," the minister prayed.

"Amen," the congregation answered in reverent unison.

The service continued. George listened, but it was difficult to pay attention to the minister's words when his mind kept wandering. He wondered what had happened on Taavi's ship. The radio often brought news of the Japanese warplanes that would nosedive into the ships. They also dropped bombs from above. And storms occasionally swept sailors out to sea. It was hard not to wonder what had gone so terribly wrong on that ship.

♦ ♦ ♦

There hadn't been a burial. There wasn't a gravesite to visit or lay flower wreaths upon. Yesterday was the funeral, yet George was still clinging to a tiny bit of hope that maybe the Western Union man had been wrong. Maybe the telegram had gotten mixed up, and it was another soldier's family that should have been notified.

The only other way of proof was to wait for the official death notice to be printed in the newspaper. The newspaper received its casualty reports directly from the government. Once it was printed, there wasn't any room for dispute.

Father always purchased the Finnish newspapers. While those printed the death notices, they just got them secondhand from the English paper, and sometimes mistakes happened during the translation process. George wanted the official list.

He went upstairs to his bedroom, opened his dresser drawer, and grabbed the sock that kept his money safe. He reached into the toe and pulled out the crisp one-dollar bill that was still tucked away from the potato harvest last fall. While he could think of a million ways to spend the dollar, he knew none of them would be worth more than the hope that maybe Taavi could come home after all.

He looked at the one-dollar bill, crossed his fingers, then folded it in half and went to Mr. Jenkins's grocery store.

"Good day, George. How are you holding up?"

Many people asked that question now. There were no more questions such as, *"How are you?"* or, *"What have you been up to?"* Now, they asked if he was okay and how he was holding up.

"Fine," he said. Though he was not fine.

"Your mother needs something?" Mr. Jenkins guessed.

"No, sir, not today. I'd like a copy of *The Tribune*, please." He pushed his dollar across the counter.

"Here you go." Mr. Jenkins handed him a newspaper and a handful of coins in exchange for the dollar.

George went outside and sat on the curb. He opened the newspaper and turned to the section that listed the death notices of the local soldiers who had lost their lives in the war. He scanned the list of names. Taavi's wasn't there. He held his breath. Maybe the telegram had been a mistake after all. Maybe it wasn't true. But then, he noticed the death dates. Still three days prior to Taavi's. The newspaper was slow in its reporting.

Every day after school for the rest of the week, George took a five-cent piece from his money stash and bought *The Tribune*. He sat on the curb and scanned the ever-growing list of names. For three days, he didn't see Taavi's name. For three days, he brought the newspaper home and deposited it in the kindling box so Mother could use it to start another fire in the hearth.

It was raining on the fourth day, so he tucked the newspaper under his arm and ran home. He spread it on the pine table in the kitchen. He ran his finger down the endless list of names, looking for those dated April 29, 1944. Name after name passed under his fingertip.

And then he stopped.

There it was. In bold, black ink.

Taavi. KIA. 29 April 1944.

George clenched his fingers into tight fists.

Stupid Hitler. Stupid Hitler and his stupid war and the stupid Japanese who joined his stupid side. Stupid. Stupid. Stupid.

He knew Mother would disapprove if he said those things out loud, so instead, he said them over and over again in his head, trying to make the hurt go away.

Stupid Japanese and their stupid planes that they stupidly flew into the American ships and bases. Stupid bombs. Stupid guns. Stupid everything. But most of all, he thought, stupid war that still held onto his other brother, Albert.

He wished Albert could come home now. They had suffered enough. The war needed to stop.

Father entered the room. George couldn't look at him. He didn't want Father to see the tears pricking at his eyes. Instead, he used his fingernail to scratch the newspaper, trying to remove the black ink that was firmly adhered to the page.

It was no use. Taavi really was dead. The Western Union man's telegram had said so. And now, the government records in the newspaper confirmed it.

He crumpled up the paper. He didn't want to see it anymore. He didn't want to see those cruel words typed on the thin paper.

KIA. 29 April 1944.

George felt strong hands on his shoulders.

"Ah, George," his father said, "your mother will want to read that."

"Not today, Father. Today, it will make her cry again."

"I see. But it's no use to hide from the truth."

"I don't want to see Mother cry anymore."

Father sat down on the bench on the other side of the table and looked him in the eye. He spoke in his soft and steady tone.

"Someday, a long time from now, you'll understand the pain your mother is going through. Someday, when you have your own wife and children and family, you'll understand. Until then, you let her have her tears. They will end. It will take time, but she will end her tears when she is ready."

George fiddled with Taavi's pencil in his pocket. Now, it seemed so futile, so childish, to have thought both of his brothers would make it home alive.

He left Father sitting alone at the table and sprinted out of the house and into the barn. He ran across the dirt floor to Taavi's workbench and tore at the map. His hands clawed at the paper, tearing it to shreds.

Stupid war. No matter what progress the Allies made, it wouldn't matter. His brother would never be able to come home.

He picked up the pieces and crumpled them into a ball. Then, he ran down the street to the dam. He stood on top of the embankment, where he and his brothers had spent so much time at the swimming hole in years past. It seemed like just yesterday that he was diving in with Taavi and Robert after their day of harvesting vegetables from the garden, scrubbing the dirt from their skin.

He dropped the crumpled map to the ground and reached into his pocket for Taavi's pencil. He turned it over and over in his hands, and then he hurled it as far as he could into the dark water. It made a small splash and sank unceremoniously to the depths below. Ripples reached the embankment, nudging the small grasses that sprouted from the shoreline.

Then, he picked up the map and threw that into the water as well. It floated for a moment, soaking up water until it became too heavy, and then it slipped silently beneath the surface.

George tried to push the thought from his head, but it wouldn't go away. He kept imagining Taavi's lifeless body sinking and swirling in the deep, dark ocean.

He fell to his knees on the earthen ground, buried his head in his hands, and cried.

And even though he had promised to be strong, he knew Taavi would be okay with these tears.

26

D-Day
June 1944

For an entire month, the oven remained cold. Not a loaf of bread was baked. Not a hot supper was made. Not even a kettle of water was heated for tea.

Mother lay in bed most days. Occasionally, George would see her in the rocking chair. But even then, her eyes were vacant and her hands were still. The usual mending and knitting had long since been tucked away in a basket near the hearth.

The house remained unusually silent. Father left for work in the wee hours of the morning, every day but Sunday. The older girls had returned to Detroit. George and his siblings were done with school for the year, and they were working what odd jobs they could find to make extra money. This meant asking the neighbors if they needed help with anything, such as hauling wood, cleaning chicken coops, or weeding gardens.

Mother remained a shell of her usual bustling self, bedridden with grief.

The laundry was done, in a fashion. The girls did the best they could without Mother's guidance. Even George and Robert helped scrub and rinse the dirty clothes.

The root cellar was nearly empty. There were only a few

miscellaneous jars of vegetables left on the shelves. Thankfully, Mr. Jenkins extended their credit at the grocery store so George could pick up some necessities. He paid Mr. Jenkins the two dollars he usually gave Mother from his paper route earnings. But he knew it was barely enough to make a dent in what they owed.

"Don't worry about it, son," Mr. Jenkins said as he updated the grocery tab. "Your mother is an honest woman. She'll get it straightened out in no time. You just let her rest right now."

Will brought over a large parcel of smoked fish with his most recent egg delivery. The ladies from town were still bringing over food, though it was slowing in quantity. George did what he could to keep the pantry stocked and organized for some semblance of meals during the long days.

He missed Mother. He knew she wasn't gone, but she certainly was not present. Her humming and singing didn't drift through the house anymore.

"Be patient," Father told the children one evening as they ate smoked fish and hard-boiled eggs for supper. "Your mother's heart has been broken. She needs time to heal."

♦ ♦ ♦

It was the morning of the first Tuesday in June when George went to the field on the other side of the railroad tracks. In a few short weeks, it was going to be his thirteenth birthday. He wondered if Mother would remember.

He walked through the tall grasses that swayed gently in the breeze. The early summer wildflowers had recently burst into bloom, bringing life to the grasslands and forests. He knelt, examining a tiny purple flower. He thought of Mother, and how she always loved seeing the fields bloom to life. He began to pick the flowers, all different hues of purple and white and pink and yellow. He picked until his hands were full, then returned home.

"Mother?" He knocked softly on the door to her bedroom.

Silence.

"Mother?" he asked again, waiting for her response.

There was none, so he gently turned the knob and nudged the door open. Mother was there, lying flat on her back under the blankets, staring at the ceiling.

"Mother, are you okay?"

She turned her head. Her usually rosy cheeks were pale. Her voice croaked when she spoke.

"No, Yrjö, I am not okay. I don't know that I'll ever be okay again. I am just so sad."

George stood in the doorway for a moment.

"I brought you these. The fields have bloomed extra beautiful this year."

Mother slowly pushed the blankets down and sat up in bed, leaning against the headboard.

"*Kiitos, rakas Yrjö*," she said. *Thank you, dear George.* She motioned for him to sit.

George perched on the edge of the bed, handing Mother the bouquet of wildflowers.

"They're beautiful," she said, smelling the sweet blossoms.

They sat in silence for a moment. George didn't know what to say.

"Sorry I've been such a bad mother these past few weeks," she said, tears welling in her eyes.

"Don't cry, Mother," said George. "You've cried so much. We're worried about you. And Father says you need to rest. Even Mr. Jenkins said you need rest. Don't worry about us. We are taking care of ourselves just fine."

"You are my sweet children," she said, pulling George close.

"I don't like seeing you so sad, Mother. I wish I could help."

"Oh, my sweet boy. You don't need to worry about helping anything. No one can bring Taavi back, and that's the only thing that could possibly heal this heartbreak."

They sat again for a moment.

"Do you think you'd like to take a walk and see the fields?" George asked, hopeful. "The sun is shining but it's not too hot yet."

She thought for a moment.

"Yes. Yes, I would like that."

George's heart leaped with joy. This was the most Mother had moved since the funeral. They walked, albeit slowly, down the street, over the railroad tracks, and to the field where the wildflowers bloomed. The morning sun had risen enough to cut through the dew, bringing forth a serene beauty before them.

"I've always loved this field so much," Mother said as they stopped to take in the view. "It reminds me of home, of Finland. Back on my father's farm, if you walked down the hill and across the river, there was a field very much like this one. And it was filled just as full of wildflowers in the summertime. Ah, I miss it so much some days. I wish it wasn't so far away."

"Sometimes do you wish you had never come to America? Do you wish you had stayed in Finland and were still with your family?"

He didn't say it out loud, but he knew if she had stayed in Finland, she wouldn't be experiencing the heartbreak that she was now.

"No, Yrjö." She ruffled his hair. "I'm so happy I moved, even if it meant leaving my family. I got to sail across the ocean so vast and blue. I got to ride a train across this beautiful country of ours. It was the adventure of a lifetime. It certainly hasn't come without its share of trials. When I moved to this country, I never could have dreamed that it would take my boys from me. America is the most wonderful country in the world, but I'd be lying if I said she hasn't been cruel to me."

She gazed across the field with a faraway look in her eyes. Then, she continued. "America has given me my greatest blessings, and now it seems she is taking them back. But I'll never regret coming here. For, without America, I wouldn't have your father, or you, or any of my sweet children."

She kissed his hair. Perhaps Father had been right. She just needed to cry her tears, and she would stop when she was ready.

As they walked back to the house, George realized he was now almost as tall as Mother. So much had happened in the past year. It seemed like a lifetime ago that he had walked to Mr.

Jenkins's grocery store wishing for something so simple as butter.

As they entered the house, Mother did something she hadn't done in over a month. She lit a fire in the stove.

"Would you like some tea?" she asked, a soft smile lighting up her eyes.

♦ ♦ ♦

"Did you hear? Did you hear?" John burst through the door as George was sipping green tea from his mug.

"Hear what? What's wrong?" Mother asked from her seat across the table.

"Turn on your radio! The Allies have landed in Normandy! They landed early this morning. We're going to win this war!"

John ran into their living room and switched on the radio for them all to hear. The static ran for a moment, and John fiddled with the dial until he found the proper news station.

"This is CBS radio," the newsman said. "As we have been reporting, earlier this morning, the Allied troops have entered into a momentous hour in world history. This is the invasion of Hitler's Europe, the zero hour. Our men have landed, beginning the push of the German lines back. We have confirmed the Allies have landed in the Normandy area of France. We will continue to keep you updated as information crosses the Atlantic."

"Oh, dear. Oh, my," Mother breathed, her hand covering her mouth.

"See? We're going to win! We're going to win this war!" John whooped and hollered, giving George a high five, and then Mother.

George was giddy with laughter. First, because he had never seen Mother give a high five, and second, because the Allies were going to win the war!

America would win, and Albert would come home!

"Go find your siblings and make sure they know of the good news," Mother said.

George and John ran first to the swimming hole to tell Robert and his friends about the invasion of Normandy. Next, they went to Aunt Elvie's house where Mary, Catherine, and Eva were helping with the spring cleaning. They had already heard the news and were gathered around the radio, the spring cleaning long since forgotten.

"Isn't this the best news we've had in ages?" Eva asked.

"That means Albert can come home soon!" George said with excitement.

"Well, we must not get our hopes up too quickly," Aunt Elvie cautioned. "This is only the beginning of the invasion of France. Our men still have a lot of work to do, but this is most definitely a turning point in the war."

Lastly, George and John stopped in the bakery where George's father worked.

"Father, did you hear?" he asked, peering over the tall glass counter.

"I did," he said with a smile. "What wonderful news."

"Do you think that means Albert can come home?"

"I reckon he still has some mighty battles to fight. But we can certainly start looking forward to the end of the war if this invasion proves successful. It's too early to know the outcome just yet."

George knew he shouldn't get his hopes up, but as he and John ran home to grab their fishing poles, he felt as light as a feather thinking about the possibility of the war ending and Albert coming home soon.

That night, the family was glued to the radio as more and more information about the invasion of Normandy poured into the broadcast system. The Allies had landed on five beaches in northern France. Casualties were mounting, and the fighting was continuing well into its second day. President Roosevelt was going to address the nation later that night.

"Can we please stay up?" the children begged in unison. "Please?"

"Yes," Mother laughed. "We haven't had this much excitement in a while. In fact, why don't we have a little party to celebrate?"

"Hurray!" they cheered.

George smiled. So did the rest of his siblings. It was good to see Mother returning to her normal self. She was wearing her cream and pink floral dress, the one that made her blue eyes sparkle a little brighter than usual. Her hair was pulled back into a bun, not a stray hair in sight. It was a welcome change from the wrinkly bedclothes and limp hair that she'd been wearing for the past month. She still had hints of sadness in her eyes, and they often caught her glancing at Taavi's portrait propped up on the mantle, but she had happiness in her spirit again.

Mother bustled about the kitchen, stoking the stove with wood and preparing a small bowl of strawberries that Catherine had picked earlier in the day.

"The berries are still quite young," Mother said, "but they'll work for a pie. It just might be a little tart."

"Do we have any sugar to sweeten them up?" Catherine asked.

"Yes, we have just a pinch, but it'll do. I'll have to talk to Mr. Jenkins tomorrow to see when another shipment will be arriving. Hopefully, I can get a ration."

Father put the coffee pot on the stove to percolate. Catherine and Mary set the table. George, Robert, and Eva crowded around the radio.

Late into the evening, they ate strawberry pie, played Monopoly and checkers, and listened to the radio until, finally, President Roosevelt came on the broadcast.

"My fellow Americans," he began. "Last night, when I spoke with you about the fall of Rome, I knew at that moment that troops of the United States and our Allies were crossing the Channel in another and greater operation. It has come to pass with success thus far."

George silently pumped his fist under the table.

"And so, in this poignant hour, I ask you to join with me in prayer." Roosevelt continued his speech, asking for guidance of the troops and strength to continue fighting the enemy onward toward victory.

George had a difficult time falling asleep that night. He wished he could see what was happening overseas on the beaches of Normandy. He wished he could ask Albert what was going on. And most of all, he hoped that Albert was safe and would be able to fight quickly, so he could come home soon.

27

Home at Last
June 1944

George nearly ran into Ricky McClain as he burst out of the post office. They both halted in their tracks. George half expected Ricky to slug him, but instead, Ricky extended his hand.

"Sorry about your brother. And—and about those things I said in school. I didn't mean them. I'm sorry."

George reached out and shook his hand. A lump formed in his throat and he couldn't say anything as he was yet again reminded that Taavi wasn't ever going to come home.

"I never did get the chance to thank your father for, you know . . ."

George nodded. He knew. Ricky didn't have to explain any further.

"Well," said Ricky after they stood in uneasy silence for a moment, "see you around."

"See you," George said.

He had just finished his paper route. Now that school was out for the summer, he started his route in the morning instead of after class. Every day after he was done, he stopped by the post office. There was a reason why he had been in such a hurry to get home. They had another letter.

"Mother!" He banged the door open.

"Oh, my, child. What is it?"

"It's another letter. From Albert."

Mother took the letter from him, tearing it open at once.

"Aren't we going to wait for Father?"

Mother's eyes were already scanning the words on the page.

"Oh," she gasped, putting her hand to her forehead and sitting down at the kitchen table.

"What's wrong?"

She broke down in great sobs. Tears poured from her eyes as her body shook. George slipped the letter from her hands and read the small words scrawled across the page.

It is time to go home.

Home! Albert was coming home!

George could hardly believe the words on the page.

"Do you think this is true?" he whispered to his mother.

Mother didn't respond. Her voice had been overtaken by tears.

Later that afternoon, when Father came home from work, George read him the letter in its entirety. It was dated June 9, 1944. Or, as the radio announcers called it, D-plus-three-Day. Albert started the letter by hoping the family was healthy and enjoying the early summer. He said he didn't have much time to write, but he had made it to a place of peace on the battlefield:

I am getting a little rest, which is well needed after our invasion of the beaches. It's not over yet, but the men are making great progress. Hopefully, by the time you get this letter, they will have swept over the ridge and into France.

General Patton came to visit those of us here. He even shook my hand and was impressed with my fighting. He said that I had done enough, that it is time to go home. If all goes according to plan, I will arrive within a few weeks.

George hadn't discussed the contents of the letter with Mother. She had been crying with joy, and he didn't want to ruin her happy spirits. But he knew he could ask Father.

"That means he's injured, right?"

"I believe so, Yrjö. Patton wouldn't let any of his men go home so easily, especially not during such a critical turning point of the war."

George looked at Mother, who was busy humming in the kitchen as she braided bread dough into a loaf. Father followed his eyes.

"It would be best not to mention anything to your mother. It's no use worrying her. She will find out soon enough. And by the date of this letter, it seems Albert should be home any day now."

George felt his stomach flutter with excitement.

♦ ♦ ♦

Nearly two weeks had passed since the date of Albert's letter. Mother was constantly looking out the window and peering down the street, waiting for her son to appear. She walked to the train station nearly every time one screeched into town.

The family was eating supper one evening when a knock at the back door broke the din of conversation.

The door creaked open.

"Hello?" called a familiar, deep voice. "Anybody home?"

"ALBERT!"

The family burst from the table, rushing to the back door.

There was laughing and crying and hugs and more tears.

"You're home! You're home!" Mother kept kissing his cheeks and hugging him, refusing to let go.

Albert laughed, "I'm home."

George was so happy he felt like he just might burst. Relief flooded through him, grateful that Albert was safely home and far away from the dangerous battlefields of war.

"Come in, come in. Supper's hot. You look like you could use a few hearty meals. My, did they feed you in that army?" Mother fretted over his state.

Albert grabbed a cane from the railing on the back steps and hobbled to the table. George's stomach sank. In all the excitement of welcoming him home, he hadn't seen the battle wounds. Mother saw it now, too.

"My sweet boy, what has happened?" she asked in pained anguish, a line of worry creasing between her eyes.

"Just a little shrapnel to the leg. Nothing a little rest won't cure. The doctors already worked their magic. But they said I wasn't going to be of any use fighting over there anymore. Sent me packing back to this side of the Atlantic."

◆ ◆ ◆

The family sat with Albert long into the night and listened to his stories of Europe, the places he had visited, and the people he had met. He told of the towns and cities they had helped liberate. How the people would run outside and hug the soldiers as they came to free them. Little children offered them gifts, sometimes even their last belongings, as heartfelt gestures of thanks. Albert said he could never accept the gifts as such but would sometimes trade money or food for their offerings.

"This one is for you." He handed it to George. It was a circular disk with a long string attached. "It's called a yo-yo."

He watched as Albert slipped a small loop at the end of the string over his finger and then tossed the disk toward the ground. It reached the end of the string and spun so fast it turned into a circular blur. Then, he snapped his wrist and the disk climbed the string back to his hand.

"The children over there could do all kinds of tricks. I traded some coins for this one. Happy birthday," he said with a smile. "Thirteen is a big year."

"Thank you," George said as he reached for the yo-yo to give it a try. He tossed it toward the ground where it wobbled and got tangled up. He was so giddy to have Albert home that he couldn't concentrate on the proper motion to keep the yo-yo spinning.

"You'll get the hang of it," Albert reassured him. "Just practice."

Mother refilled coffee cups as they talked, her face alternating between elation when she looked at Albert and grief when she looked at Taavi's photograph on the mantle.

George couldn't take his eyes off Albert's face as his older brother relayed news from across the ocean. It seemed like a lifetime ago that they were sending Albert off to war. He had been just a boy then, only weeks out of his high school graduation, when he left on the train. Now, his features were hardened. His jaw was strong and set. Lines creased his face between his eyebrows. He spoke slower, now more cautious and deliberate in his word choice.

It seemed like they had all aged a decade in the past year. George felt his boyishness falling by the wayside. Too much had happened to still be so young. So much pain and heartbreak. The tearing apart of their family by the war. Two brothers had left but only one came back. His older sisters no longer lived at home. He knew things would never be the same as they had been on his twelfth birthday.

He would have to adjust to the new normal. It would take time, but just like Albert's leg, the pain from the wounds of the war would dim. Scars both inside and out would always remain, but the intense, crushing pain in his family's hearts would gradually diminish.

That night, two brothers climbed the stairs while the third hobbled up with the help of a cane. Without saying a word, and even though they were much too big and Albert was in pain, they all crawled into the same bed.

This was their family now. Three brothers. The fourth gone from the world but still very much alive in their hearts and memories. George imagined Taavi looking down from his place in

Heaven above, a smile tugging at the corners of his mouth as he watched his three brothers squish into one small bed for the night.

EPILOGUE
A Uniformed Visitor
October 1945

It had been over a year since Albert had come home. The Allies had gained their victory in Europe in May. Hitler's war had come to a close. In August, the Allies had gained their final victory in the Pacific. The war was officially over.

Even though the battles overseas were finished, the war left its scars on the world, and George, too. He lay awake many nights staring out at the starry sky as he waited for Albert's nightmares to subside. Albert tossed and turned in his sleep, crying out for his fellow soldiers left behind on the battlefields of Europe, never remembering it in the morning but always unrested come daylight.

George never asked questions. Those invisible battle scars were something Albert never spoke about. He told the family stories of the places he had visited and the people he had met, but he never talked about the darkness of war or those things that caused him to thrash about at night.

Now, it was late October once again, the season of harvesting and preparing for the winter ahead.

George was fourteen. He was in the ninth grade and had just finished up his first season on the high school football team. They hadn't made the playoffs, but nonetheless, he was happy with their record of five wins and four losses.

The girls had moved back home from Detroit. The war factories had closed down or had begun to make other goods instead of bombs and tanks.

Helena's attempts to catch the fancy of Mr. Tinney had proved successful, and they were now married, with a baby on the way. Elaine and Ann were working, both soon to be married to their own beaus.

The girls had brought back more than enough money to purchase a washing machine for Mother. She still had to hang the wet clothes on the clothesline outside to dry, but that was hardly any work at all compared to the heavy lifting she used to do on laundry day.

Catherine had graduated from high school. The only family members left in school now were Mary, Eva, George, and Robert.

Earlier that summer, the city had updated their street with plumbing infrastructure. Father installed an indoor toilet in the washroom, so they no longer had to use the outhouse in the backyard. Lefty and Cruz had stopped by one last time to pump the outhouse clean before Father filled in the pit and tore down the small, wooden structure. George, Robert, and Albert certainly enjoyed the extra space in the yard when they played pass with a football or baseball.

Albert was working as a delivery driver for the post office. He drove their big, white mail truck to every town in a hundred-mile radius, delivering parcels and packages. His leg still bothered him, but he was grateful that he was able to sit down for much of the time at his job.

The doctors had taken out as much of the shrapnel as they could, but some pieces were lodged too deep to safely remove.

"It just doesn't want to work like it used to," he said one day, limping inside the house for supper. "I can tell a storm's a'brewing. The ol' souvenirs in my leg can feel a change in the weather many days out."

"Good thing the rest of the garden was harvested last week," Mother commented.

The family passed heaping platters of food around the table. George filled his plate. He had long since passed Mother in height and was now working on catching up with Albert. In the way of most young, growing boys, this meant he had a ravenous appetite.

"Save some for the rest of us, Yrjö," Mother said with a twinkle in her eyes.

"Sorry, ma'am," he said as he put back a scoop of mashed potatoes.

Knock, knock, knock.

The family froze. No one moved a muscle.

Knock, knock, knock.

It came from the front door. The last visitor that had knocked on the front door was the Western Union man. And there was no reason for him to be visiting anymore. Besides, anyone could telephone them now instead of sending a telegram. They had had one installed in the kitchen over the summer.

"Now, just who could that be?" Mother asked under her breath as she rose to answer the door.

The family watched wide-eyed as Mother pulled it open. In

stepped a uniformed sailor.

"Pardon my abruptness, ma'am. I needed to take a visit here on my way home."

Mother opened her mouth, but words didn't come out.

"Forgive me, ma'am, the name's Freedom. Robert Freedom."

"Well, isn't that just a fine name for a sailor," Mother said, recovering her voice. "Come join us for supper. We only just started."

"No, I best be on my way. Didn't mean to interrupt. Besides, my folks are certainly waiting for me. Got a few hours' train ride to get where I'm going. Took the long way to stop here."

He stepped into the kitchen, removed his hat, and nodded to the family gathered around the table.

"I knew your son, ma'am," he said. "Taavi. We enlisted together, and it just so happens the Good Lord saw fit to ship us off together. He was the strongest sailor I ever knew. Hard worker. Never heard a complaint from him no matter how long the day. You have my deepest sympathies, ma'am. His loss was hard on our crew. It was the first of its sort. Many came after, but there's something about the first one that does a man in."

Mother nodded, her eyes clouding up with tears as the man spoke of Taavi.

"He worked as a fireman, as did I. Most of our time was spent below deck making sure the engines and mechanical systems weren't going to go up in flames. But when the call came, and enemy warplanes and ships came into range, we had to rush up on deck and take up our position at a gun. We had practiced and practiced. Mock scenarios and the like.

"But it was nothing anyone could have prepared for. A swarm of Japanese planes came overhead. Dropping bombs like it was nobody's business. Thought the whole ship was going to go under. Took me a moment to realize what had happened. The smoke and noise were something fierce.

"I looked down, and I'm sorry to say he was already gone. There was nothing anyone could have done. If it's any reassurance to you, he never suffered."

Mother grabbed the sailor's arm, and he helped her to her rocking chair.

"Again, ma'am, so sorry to burst in on you. But I had to let you know. It's been on my mind. Before we set sail, we promised each other that if something happened, we'd let the other's family know. So, that's why I came—per his request, ma'am. And also to give you these."

Robert Freedom reached into his pocket and pulled out three items.

"They were his. I was able to retrieve them before we laid him to rest the following day."

Mother turned the items over in her hands, tears streaming down her cheeks. George looked around the table, and all the girls had tears in their eyes. Father, too.

Then she stood and passed them around the table for the family to see. George held the items in his hands, treasuring one last piece of Taavi. First were his Navy-issued tags, with his name and identifying information embossed into the metal. Next was a half-written letter addressed to the family, telling them of his journey across the ocean so far. It was dated the day prior to his death. The last item passed around the table was a folded-in-half photograph of Mother and Father.

"Well, ma'am, sir," the sailor said as he nodded his head politely at George's parents and then the rest of the family. "I best be going now. I have a train to catch and don't want to keep you any longer. You have my prayers for peace. Your son was a wonderful man. You should be very proud of him and his sacrifice. And as we can see now, thankfully, it wasn't in vain."

He shook Mother's hand, and just as quickly as he came, Robert Freedom walked out of the house and was swallowed up by the night.

Author's Note

It's difficult to pinpoint the exact moment when the idea for *When War Knocks* came to be. One could argue it started back before I even knew what a writer was, when the earliest memories of my grandpa were forming. Inspiration also came from a lifetime of his love and support, along with his vivid stories of navigating life as a first-generation American born to Finnish immigrant parents. As time went on and I heard more stories, I had a desire to capture and write them down. However, I didn't know how to undertake such a daunting task.

Many of the stories he told were of his early adult years. Seasons spent steering freighters on the Great Lakes. Working in the copper mines. Even a stint as an ambulance driver and assistant to the funeral director. (That's a story guaranteed to make anyone laugh until they cry!)

Time marched on, and my mind remained completely void of any idea as to how to appropriately capture Grandpa's adventures. I pondered a biography, a memoir, and adult fiction. The more I thought about the task at hand, the more I wanted to turn off the part of my brain that desired to write the story, as it seemed impossible to get it right.

Then, in the spring of 2019, a spark of an idea burrowed into my mind. I realized there was an air of innocence about his stories. I found myself wanting to tell his story through the eyes of young George, and from there, the idea for a middle-grade historical fiction novel began to form. And so began the research. I reread historical fiction books that I had enjoyed as a child. I watched WWII documentaries. I bought, borrowed, and read articles and books about Finnish immigrants growing up in Michigan's Copper Country. I spent time in the genealogy room at the library researching family and WWII history.

Yet, there was only one person who could tell his story best and help me put the words on the page: Grandpa. So, I began to compile a list of questions that would help me paint a picture of his life as a young boy growing up in Calumet, Michigan. Originally, I had planned to interview him in October of 2019, on a pre-scheduled trip to where he now lived, almost 1,000 miles away. But the fates guided me differently, and they told me that I needed to get to him sooner. So, in August of 2019, I took a few days off work and drove nine hours to his vacation home to visit.

Grandpa was the best sport during the interview. He patiently answered all 280 questions. We talked for two and a half hours, and I got to listen to him reminisce about what he liked to call "the good old days." For those two and a half hours, I asked question after question and typed out his responses while recording our conversation. He gave me all the information I needed to get started in bringing the character of twelve-year-old George to life. And so, I began outlining and drafting the novel. I was preparing a second round of interview questions, as the first batch had barely scratched the surface once I started to get into the details of the story.

But as time stops for no one, mine with Grandpa had run out.

Six weeks after that first and only interview, in September of

2019, I received a devastating phone call from my dad. Grandpa had passed away.

In the weeks that followed, I waded through the grief. A journey of creating this story that I started with Grandpa now had to be finished alone. I will be forever grateful that I recorded that last conversation I had with him. It took over a month before I could go back and listen to it again. But when I did, I laughed, I cried, and, more than ever, I wanted to share his story.

So, I began writing again. I did the best I could to bring George and his supporting characters to life. Many elements of this story are based on fact. Most of the character names and places have been changed, but some remain true to maintain the historical integrity of the story. Many of the events are based on actual happenings from Grandpa's life, though pieces of the timeline have been rearranged to fit the pacing of this novel. However, being a work of historical fiction, some of the people, places, and events are exaggerated, altered to fit the narrative of the story, or completely fictitious.

Throughout the writing process, I came to love and appreciate a George that I had never even thought of before. To me, he was always "Old Grandpa." (Let's be honest, to a child, anyone over 30 is ancient!) No matter how much older I got, he was always "my old grandpa," and I never gave it much thought that he, too, was at one point a carefree little boy. How wrong I was to never question his childhood. He had a vibrant and wonderful tale to tell.

And so became *When War Knocks*, a story of a young boy

losing his innocence to the indiscriminate outcomes of war. I wish he was here to read it, to give advice on what needed to be changed, and to answer the thousands of questions that I had to ask the internet while writing this story.

Instead, I'm comforted knowing that he is looking down from the heavens above, perhaps enjoying a warm slice of heavenly apple pie and catching up on decades of lost time with a brother he hasn't seen since childhood.

I hope this book has been an enjoyable read.

But most of all, Grandpa, I hope I've done justice to your story.

Acknowledgements

Though writing in and of itself is a solitary journey, writing a book is anything but a road traveled alone. I have many thanks to give, and I know I will never be able to repay everyone for your time and patience as you helped bring this story to life.

First and foremost, thank you to anyone who read this book. Because of you, Grandpa's story lives on.

Thank you to Mike Ball and the rest of the BDL's writers' group. Your unwavering support, encouragement, and advice over the years have been invaluable. I never could have dreamed my journey would take me here when I walked into that room five years ago.

And speaking of the BDL, thank you to the staff for lending your time and resources in the genealogy room. The historical accuracies would not have been possible without your services. Mark, you may not remember me, but I'll never forget your help.

To Auntie Ruth, your love and support were instrumental in keeping me going. Thank you for the "Intro to Finn" lessons via text and email. (Any inaccuracies in the story are solely the fault of the student!) I'll appreciate you always.

To Auntie Teresa, for the wise words that eventually became the dedication line of this book.

To the rest of my "Grandpa George" family: parents, brothers, aunts, uncles, cousins, nieces, and nephews—thank you for being such a gracious family and making so many wonderful memories throughout the years. Though we may not always see each other often, each one of you has in some way shaped me into the person I am today.

Thank you to the team of professionals who offered their expertise in crafting this book: L. Austen Johnson, for your hand in copyediting, cover design, and general guidance on the publishing process. Lydia Redwine, for thoughtful comments and suggestions as a beta reader. Megan Basinger at Fine Fuse Editorial Services, for being the final set of eyes in the proofreading stage. Coralie Kivisto, for bringing the cover art to life. Thank you to all, I couldn't have done it alone.

To other authors who have forged this path ahead of me, thank you for putting your books into the universe so I could become inspired. Keep on writing; there are more stories to be told.

Thank you to my husband, for your support as I continue on this writing journey. Most of all, thank you for taking care of our toddler and shooing me out of the house so I could write without hearing the unending chorus of "Mom-Mom-Mom-Mom-Mom."

To those not listed here but who still helped provide information and encouragement, thank you!

And most importantly, thank you to Grandpa. For without you, this story would never have come to be. Enjoy your wings—you've certainly earned them.

Made in the USA
Monee, IL
22 October 2020

45890228R00143